A Life on the Lane

A Tale of Life on Portobello Road W11

Melvin Wilkinson

Melvin Wilkinson

Copyright © 2019 Melvin Wilkinson

All rights reserved

ISBN-13: 9781796659450

This book is a work of fiction. Names, characters, places and incidents are either the product of the author's imagination or are used fictionally. Any resemblance to actual persons, living or dead, or to actual events is entirely coincidental.

All rights reserved. Including the right to reproduce this book or portions thereof, in any form. No part of this text may be reproduced in any form without the express written permission of the author.

CONTENTS

	Foreword	v
1	Looking back	Pg 1
2	School days	Pg 7
3	Reprisal	Pg 13
4	Life will never be the same	Pg 24
5	Not a good start	Pg 46
6	A big idea	Pg 61
7	An appointment to keep	Pg 81
8	A career in the army?	Pg 95
9	It's a good feeling	Pg 109
10	Young love	Pg 123
11	Getting formal	Pg 139
12	The precious things	Pg 152
13	Changes	Pg 157
14	Grown up feeling	Pg 169
15	Moving on	Pg 182
16	New beginning	Pg 188
17	A fitting end	Pg 197
	Acknowledgements	Pg 205
	About the Author	Pg 206

Melvin Wilkinson

A Life on the Lane

FOREWORD

The Royal Borough of Kensington and Chelsea wow what a title, and along with a fantastic name what a place. It's a Marmite type of area really; everyone that has anything to do with it will either fall in love or simply hate the place. As I said from the very first page of this book the Royal Borough was "friend and family to me and on the other hand a foe that nearly killed and made me suffer almost beyond the boundaries of human endurance" but I still love the place. I return regularly to just wander around the Lane or streets, to mingle with west Londoners, west Londoners from all over the world.

This book is a work of fiction but everything within its pages is based on fact. Anyone that was around the area in the 1950s 60s or 70s will be able to recognise themselves or someone they know, they will have had experiences the same as Malc or Sue, they will have heard of tragedies like that which hit Eric and his family.

Within the streets of Notting Hill and Dale people suffered on a daily basis, even for me and my family who were probably better off than many we felt the reality of poverty and pain. We lived cheek by jowl with those that suffered but put up a fight against their conditions. It was the people of W11/10 that eventually changed how tenants were treated; it was of course those very people that suffered at the hands of Peter Rachman and Michael de Freitas et al. It was Rachman himself that was made immortal by the fact that Rachmanism became a word to be found in the English language, it's a noun in the Oxford English dictionary meaning the intimidation and exploitation of tenants by an unscrupulous landlord.

That said the lives of so many people were very hard but it was a great life as well, with the law as it is today children cannot get life's experiences the way we did by doing a bit of work on the lane. They cannot mix with people the way we did because of the fear of their parents wanting to protect them.

It's a dichotomy that we say children grow up too quickly these days but do they, are they streetwise or in possession of a degree from the university of life, I for one am not sure they do, I am also not sure who is to blame if anyone.

Well with that out of the way it would be nice if you enjoy this little tale, I hope you recognise some of the situations described within its pages, I also feel sure you will recognise some of the characters either good or bad and whether good or bad they all made up the population of this very special part of London.

A Life on the Lane

vii

CHAPTER 1
LOOKING BACK

Today was going to be a long one, not just long because I knew what to expect and wanted to avoid it, but long because I was putting to rest the man that taught me much and treated me like a son for as long as I could remember. I for once had to be strong, to maintain dignity, and send him off the right way.

Eric was a mountain of a man, not only in build but in presence and community standing; he had always been at the very centre of Notting Hill life. He hated to see anybody hard done by or bullied and he would do anything for anyone. He was a quiet man with secrets you could only guess at, was there pain or anger in his past, something strong that drove him through tough times in one of the poorest parts of London if not Europe?.

It's a bit of a cliché to expound on being from a tough area, you hear it all the time from East Enders how they suffered during the war but the sense of community got them through, or from Glaswegians banging on about the Gorbals and the drunken fights on Friday night, but believe me this little bit of west London can stand up there with the worst that man's congested cityscapes can throw at it.

The Notting Hill we know now with its millionaires, pop stars and aristocrats has been a friend and family to me and on the other hand a foe that has nearly killed and made me suffer, almost beyond the boundaries of human endurance. It's a place Eric had vowed never to leave and he was true to his word, he was born in W11 and in the end died in W11 and I wonder who could imagine the torture he too had suffered during his 80 something years of being a West Londoner.

We all, that were gathering for the funeral service, knew that Eric had to have a proper market traders send off and the first part of his journey to the cemetery would be on a stall holders hand barrow before being transferred to the hearse and driven out of Portobello Road and indeed out of W11 for the last time. You see Eric had been a stall holder for more years than I care to remember and it was Eric that had given me a Saturday job dressing the veg for his stall and collecting his tea from the market cafe in a white enamelled jug, they were hard times but we all enjoyed the costermonger's camaraderie.

Market people have a wicked sense of humour and the lads that worked the market on a Saturday so often bore the brunt of their practical jokes, they were harmless really but they taught us some valuable lessons, lessons from the University of Life Eric always told me. I remember one wet Saturday being sent down to the iron mongers for a "long weight" which I assumed was to hold down the tarpaulin that kept the stall holder dry, I hadn't made the connection between weight and wait and was kept hanging around the shop for going on half an hour. It was obvious that the ironmonger had seen Saturday lads come in and ask for the same thing time and time again, and time and time again he had probably served a dozen or more customers before sending the hapless youngster back to the stall with the words "there you go was that wait long enough for you?" That was when it dawned on you exactly what was going on. When I got back to the stall Eric gave me an almighty clip round the ear for being away from my work for so long and to rub it in even more he docked me a tanner of my wages, that's sixpence in case you didn't know, which may sound a bit harsh but to be truthful I understood why he did it.

The following Monday on my way home from school I walked down the lane, that's what we called the market, Eric called me over "Oye tiddler 'ere's that tanner get yourself some sweets with it", he knew I wouldn't fall for that one again, he had succeeded in teaching me a very important lesson, it was me that didn't know what the lesson was at the time.

Eric wasn't the only one that had history in Notting Hill, I too had my moments and during the quiet time in my morning bath feeling melancholy my mind drifted back to my early days, the first term at the University of Life.

This is where my story begins in earnest, back in the very beginning of the 1960's in a time of racial unrest, a time of crime and a time of childhood ignorance to what was really important.

Back then I was almost a street urchin, I knew all the dodges and I'd seen things that a boy barely into double figures should know about let alone see and be involved in. For a start there was the prostitutes, we could earn a good bit of silver, maybe a florin or even half a dollar although more often than not a tanner or a few coppers for directing punters to the right basement. We knew the punters because they stood out like a sore thumb, they had decent cars you see, they would drive down from Chelsea looking for a little bit of excitement and we were always willing to point them in the right direction for a fee. I'm not sure I knew what was really going on but once we'd taken the gullible saps to the girl of our choice more often than not we could get a bit of a view of what was going on behind the filthy curtains of the basement dens.

I had a theory about why there was always either a gap in the curtains or more often no curtains at all, you see these girls needed to get as many men through their doors as possible and if we didn't know they were free we might direct the toffs elsewhere, and that wouldn't do would it, so we could look through the windows before sending in the next client, easy.

I quite liked the working girls and it didn't matter to me if they were black or white, young or old they were in the same boat as us, always watching their backs, scared their pimps would be unhappy with their productivity, you see even though most of us knew our place and were resigned to just doing what we had to, to get by, some other people would use whatever means necessary to claw their way out of the gutter or in our case the slums. That's why there were people like "Peter the Pole" and Michael Delgardo, people who would do anything and hurt anyone to make money and they didn't care if those people were the rich vice tourists from up west or the poor locals that were just ripe to be stripped of what little they might have.

Notting Hill is well known as a cosmopolitan area and so it has always been, we've seen them all, many come and many go and the makeup of the population changes on a regular basis, now I don't mean this to be a history lesson but let's go way back. It all started in the 1800's with the gypsies because at that time this was still a rural area and the gypsies would gather on land in the Dale, hundreds of them sometimes and of course eventually many settled that's why we have a lot of Roma words in our slang. Then there were the Irish, navies brought in to construct the railways and canals that encircle us, I'm told that navies is short for navigation workers but with my limited education that could easily be a load of old bull. Then there were the poor, our predecessors slung out and moved here because the knobs wanted Chelsea and the West End for themselves. The list goes on so I won't bore you, but one lot really made a difference to me and that was the West Indians who arrived in the 1950's.

The West Indians had it tough, very tough but they also knew how to enjoy themselves they had blues parties and Shabeens, illegal drinking clubs, and boy could they drink, not in the pubs because they were unwelcome, but in the basements and tenements of the area which was great for us kids, you see the beer came in bottles and we would grab the empties to take to the off licence and claim the deposit. That was easy money until you got caught; poor old Keith a mate of mine from school caught a quart bottle on the back of his head when one of the drinkers caught him reaching inside the door to grab just one last bottle before we went to cash in. I really felt sorry for him, it bled for ages until someone came up with the idea of putting mud on it to stop the bleeding, it's a wonder he didn't die of blood poisoning, still he got over it.

Then there was school, Colville Junior Mixed to be precise, a grand red brick Victorian building with strict matronly teachers and cold classrooms. School was never really for me, but I was always torn between the market where I felt so at home and my school desk because the one person that I could really relate to and spend all my time with sat on the next desk.

A Life on the Lane

CHAPTER 2
SCHOOL DAYS

Linda sat on the desk alongside me at school, she was the most special person I knew, she was as close as any sister to me, and if we weren't so young I might even say we loved each other. Linda was Eric's daughter so even though I had a real family of my own the Browns were like an adopted family; I had known them from the age of 3 when I went to the nursery school. Linda and I had hit it off from day one playing together and going to each others' houses whenever we could. We liked the same sweets, enjoyed doing the same things together and just being in each others' company, I can't say we ever got tired of each other and unlike most children there were very few arguments. Even then I knew we were going to be friends for life, it would be impossible to live apart.

Linda lived in a typically Notting Hill Victorian, and I use the term loosely, villa. It wasn't what you would think of as a villa these days, it was a white 4 story stucco building which had been divided into flats and bedsits. People came and went each week, and each week it seemed that they would fit more and more people in. Every inch of space was used, even the landings housed communal kitchens, and the furnished rooms had as many as 4 or 5 beds in them. People would come home from work to find another bed had been put in their room and hey presto they were sharing with a complete stranger.

The house was owned by "Peter the Pole" and it was just one of many, he specialised in housing anyone that couldn't find accommodation anywhere else. In those days it was a common sight to see signs in house windows reading "Room to let - No Blacks - No Irish - No dogs" and no one would do anything about it, except that is Peter. If you had been tramping around looking for somewhere to live Peter had the answer and as I say for the cost of another second hand bed in one of his bedsits you had somewhere to sleep.

So how did Eric and his family find themselves living in such accommodation? Well they had rented the first floor flat since before Peter had acquired it and Peter wanted them out. They had 2 rooms and a kitchen bathroom, yes that is kitchen bathroom, one small room with sink, cooker and small table at one end and a bath at the other, the toilet was shared by 2 floors and because it was shared, the toilet paper was kept in the kitchen, forgetting the paper when you went to the "loo" could be a disaster except for the fact that many of the other residents used it as a library so invariably there was a newspaper abandoned in there.

This was not a self contained flat there was no door to close to lock the rest of the residents out, there was just the bedroom door, the living room door and the kitchen door. The living room doubled as Eric and Jean's bedroom and the bedroom, small as it was, was shared by Linda and her brother Stewart.

As I said Peter wanted the Browns out, a flat that size could accommodate at least twice as many people and earn twice or three times the rent. Peter had decided they had to go so he

A Life on the Lane

started a campaign of harassment first the electric would fail at various times, there would be mysterious water leaks in the rooms above, even though there was no running water in that room, and there were the rent increases.

Linda and Stewart didn't really know what was going on, life still had too many adventures to worry about where they would live or why their bed was wet, and they just carried on blissfully unaware of the situation. Eric was working the market everyday and Jean worked as a dinner lady at the school, they were keeping their heads above water but only just. They must have been the first of the Notting Hill vegetarians, Jean could make a meal out of just about any veg that Eric brought home. I heard Mrs. Brown comment one day on the state of the vegetables Eric came home with, I could tell he was hurt, for the first time Eric raised his voice. He never shouted, he didn't need to, he could be kind and stern without changing the tone of his voice, you just knew when to laugh and when not to answer back. I'm sure that day as he passed Linda and me on the landing that Eric had a tear in his eye, because the one thing Eric feared was failure and in his mind he was beginning to fail his family.

Linda went to her mum and wanted to know what was wrong, "don't worry darling, daddy's just feeling under the weather, he'll be fine tomorrow". I saw the veg that had been thrown to the floor and even with my veg stall knowledge I could see this was the pick-ups from a closed market. Pick-ups are the damaged stuff that is tossed under the stalls during the trading day and is usually collected by the homeless or very poor after the market closes, for the proud man Eric was, he could never imagine stooping this low, it was certainly way outside his comfort zone.

Next day on my way to school Eric threw me an apple "there's your lunch tiddler; you know one of them every day keeps the doctor away". For the first time I felt guilty about taking something from Eric, I was getting a first class apple and the Browns were getting the crap.

In class Linda was her usual bubbly happy self there was no hint of the upset from the day before but for me, that apple was like a millstone around my neck, I fiddled with it all morning during lessons. It was just a matter of time before Mrs. Love the most feared teacher in school homed in on the one pupil that didn't have the faintest idea what had been going on in class, and sure enough just before playtime I got the ruler round my ear. There was nothing I could say I had not heard a word all morning, all I could hear was Eric shouting at Mrs. Brown about the vegetables. I don't know why it had affected me so deeply while Linda seemed to have completely forgotten about what had happened, maybe it was because I had seen Eric in a male dominated environment at work during which time I had seen him handle "yobs", hard men, angry housewives and thieving children at the stall, but not once had I heard him raise his voice, it just never happened. One time it became more than clear that Eric was a clever bloke and wouldn't resort to anger easily, a bolshie woman wanted a pound of apples, trouble was 4 apples came in under and 5 were over. Nine times out of ten Eric would have just given the over-weight apples but this woman got right up Eric's nose, so he cut one apple in half snatched the money and gave her the four and a half or one pound of apples, said thank you and served the next punter. I couldn't have thought that quick which is why Eric was a perfect "coster"

A Life on the Lane

The next day I was back in school again, and again Linda was all smiles and bubbly, I was better than the day before and managed to at least listen to what was going on in class, perhaps today I wouldn't attract Mrs. Love's attention and would avoid the swift sharp pain of the ruler around the back of the head.

It was a rare occasion that I was told to go with another pupil to collect the morning milk from the playground, you see in those days all school children got a small bottle of milk each morning and you only got to be milk monitor if you were one of teachers "little angels", which was not by any stretch of the imagination me. "Who is going to help bring the milk up with Malcolm?" asked Mrs. Love. Linda's hand was up in a flash and to my delight she was chosen. Now this might seem strange but the old school was built specifically to keep girls and boys apart as much as possible, and although we sat within a couple of feet of each other we never got the opportunity to talk to each other during the day. "Off you go you two be quick and use the girls staircase" snapped Mrs. Love, now what is the significance of the point she made about the stairs you might ask, well the school had 2 sets of stairs that ran up parallel to each other, one for the girls and one for the boys. The silly thing was that the staircases were not at either end of the building but right in the middle side by side, it never made sense to me but nor did a lot of mysteries of the school nor the adult world.

Linda and I happily wandered off to collect the milk from the playground and we had a few valuable minutes to talk. "Do you want to come to my house after school" I asked, I just wanted her away from her parents in case Eric kicked off again, I wasn't scared for her safety as much as not wanting her to see her father so anguished that he resorted to shouting. Linda was the apple of Eric's eye and even at my tender age could see the bond that they had; it was stronger than my own relationship with my parents and stronger than anyone else I knew. Her reply took me a back a bit I didn't expect her to say no, "why not you never say no." "Sorry" she said "but Dads going to a tenants' meeting tonight and I'm going with him, it's been arranged by Jennifer's Dad, if you want you can come too". "Yeah! Why not I won't have anything else to do, I'll come over straight after my tea" I said.

With that we had arrived at the stack of milk crates, we took our quota and trundled back up the stairs with our load. I knew we wouldn't be able to talk again until we walked home from school at 4 o'clock but I felt happier having had a few brief minutes with Linda

A Life on the Lane

CHAPTER 3
REPRISAL

"Welcome to the first meeting of the West 11 Private Residents Association", Jennifer's dad was the chairman and as such he was in control of the meeting, he was up front opening the proceedings, he too had much to complain about, much also to worry about because he had already managed cross swords with both "Peter the Pole" and his hired heavy, Michael. Michael was a West Indian well known around the Westbourne Park Road and All Saints Road area, he ran most of the working girls, controlled many of the blues parties and supplied just about anything that was either illegal or hard to come by.

Jennifer's father, Mr. Watkins continued the meeting with stories of harassment and bullyboy tactics dished out by some of the private landlords in W11, primarily amongst these were "Peter the Pole" and Michael. "They put prostitutes in rooms in the tenements we rent and they are coming and going at all times of the day and night, my wife has been harassed by their clients on a number of occasions and I'm scared for my daughter's safety" - one of the men in the audience blurted out - "but what can we do about it, we need somewhere.....!". The resident was cut off mid sentence by the slamming of the door at the back of the church hall. Framed by the door was a large black man, you didn't need to

13

see his face everyone knew exactly who this was, many had fallen foul of his temper or his cold calculated stare which said it would be silly to take any grievance any further. This was Michael, part gangster, part pimp and part celebrity, someone that was well known to the police and both the black and white communities in the area. During the race riots Michael was central in every disturbance, he was a particularly high profile face amongst the crowd in the riot that became known as the battle of Blenheim Crescent, and he was to put it in simple terms a very dangerous man.

Michael walked up one aisle and down the other looking at each individual sitting there, he didn't say a word, he didn't have to, and everybody knew exactly what Michael was doing at the meeting. He stopped briefly at the door, turned around and winked at Mr. Watkins before leaving. Well I might only be 10, I thought, but I know exactly what that little display was for and so did everyone in that room especially all those living in one of Peter's houses which Michael looked after. It was probably a waste of time but quickly and quietly many of those present slipped out of the hall sheepishly tucking their chins into the collars of their coats, if Michael knew them, their cards had been marked, and one way or another they would pay for this display of defiance. I looked at Eric, but his eye contact with Jennifer's dad never flinched, even as the speaker's voice stuttered then briefly paused, Eric's eyes moved not one bit. I couldn't help wondering how this was going to affect Linda. She knew Michael and what he was capable of as well as anyone, she had watched as Michael had got to the front of the hall and looked deeply into her dad's eyes, was she also wondering how and when her family would suffer at the hand of this thug.

A Life on the Lane

That night after the meeting was over, for the first time ever Eric treated Linda and I as children, he insisted on taking me home and waiting with me until my dad came down to the door. Linda was allowed to come in with me while our fathers spoke, the evening's events had clearly made an indelible mark on Eric, he was worried, probably for his family more than himself but nevertheless worried which was a first in the years that I had known him.

The next day was Saturday, the best day of the week; it was an early start because Saturday was a working day in the university of Portobello market. As usual I was up by seven o'clock and washed and dressed before seven thirty, well before. As with most kids of my age personal hygiene wasn't at the top of my "to do" lists, all I wanted to do was get down the lane and start dressing the veg for the day ahead. Eric always started the day with the same words, "you little bugger, don't think I'm going to start paying you till eight o'clock, you're too late to set up the stall and too bloody early to restock, now get down the café and get me a brew or you'll not start getting paid 'til nine". It didn't really make any difference I'd have done it for nothing and Eric knew that, he also knew that getting the tea from the café at that time was a lucrative sideline for me, you see I could pick up half a dozen jugs of tea in one go and each stall holder would give me a few coppers for the service. Lots of the stallholders didn't want to have Saturday lads or wouldn't pay them so I filled the gap in the market shall we say, "it's all a case of supply and demand" I used to say. I didn't actually know what that meant, I'd heard it on a radio programme once and it seemed to fit the situation.

It was a good start to the day mainly because it wasn't

raining, on a dry day the women would come out early to walk up the top end of the lane in what we called the junk market. The kids in those days didn't get designer clothes, in fact they didn't get new clothes, and as I think back it wasn't only us kids. The majority of clothing, furniture and bric-a-brac we as a community had, came from the market and some of it was to say the least unusual. Jennifer came to school once with a pair of stag antlers which she'd picked up after the market closed, they would have been on their wall if Mrs. Watkins had allowed it but she drew the line at having smelly animal remains in the house. Needless to say when she asked to have them mounted on the classroom wall it was rejected in no uncertain terms by Mrs. Love.

I preferred it when business was steady because there was more to do, it was a case of sort the apples, trim the cauliflowers or cut the bananas off the stalk, that was a job I enjoyed you see the bananas came in wooden crates straight from the boat via the ripening sheds, that meant if there were any spiders in the cargo when they left the West Indies then they were still there when they arrived in jungle W11. I kept an old cocoa tin with me for such finds, and then on Monday the arachnid would miraculously find its way into the teacher's drawer, fortunately for Mrs. Love the spiders were invariably dead.

By dinner time I was ready to be dispatched for the tea and again I would be able to use Eric's time to make a little extra money collecting for the other stallholders but this time my jaunt to the café was different. I was only a couple of stalls away from Eric's when I saw Michael and a couple of his associates heading towards our stall, I couldn't help it I had to wait and watch just in case, I knew there was nothing I could

A Life on the Lane

do and I also knew that the other market boys would stand with Eric but I knew Michael wouldn't walk past Eric without making his presence felt. Stan the fishmonger could see me and he obviously knew what had happened the night before, he tugged my ear and in no uncertain words told me to "'urry up and get the bloody Rosie lad or there ain't gonna be a tip in it for ya". When I got back Eric was agitated I knew what it was even though he didn't say anything, sometimes words just aren't needed.

Saturday was Eric's "bookie" day, not that he was a big gambler just the odd couple of bob on the "gee gee's", horses and horse racing runs deep in market people's lives, it's probably a legacy of the gypsy in them. They often looked after their cart horses better than their wives. It was only the junk people from the top end of the lane that had horses nowadays, mainly because they were nearly all rag and bone men during the week, needless to say it was easier to drive a van to Covent Garden every morning than a horse and cart.

Eric drank his tea and made his excuses leaving Paul, his assistant in charge of the stall, I watched Eric disappear into the bookies but he was different there was no spring in his step and he ignored Betty on the flower stall when she shouted a tip for the two thirty to him, that wasn't like him, everyone spoke to Eric and Eric always spoke to everyone in return.

That afternoon was the worst I've ever spent on the stall, Paul did most of the work and you could have cut the atmosphere with a knife all I wanted to do was get finished and go home for my evening meal. Tomorrow was Sunday I knew that I would play out with the boys and see Linda, and of course there would be the Salvation Army on the corner of

All Saints Road to take "the Mickey" out of. Sunday would definitely be an improvement on Saturday and I never thought I'd ever say that.

Sunday morning and its a boys' day, we always gathered over the flats play area for a morning of flat out exercise or as we called it footie. The play area faced onto Powis Gardens a non-descript road but interesting for some in that the houses had basements. As I indicated before many of the "working girls" worked out of basements and those working out of Powis Gardens answered to Michael. He was never seen around on a Sunday morning mainly because Saturday night was a busy time in Notting Hill and he was probably just going to bed when everyone was getting up, but today was different, it was only about 11am when we heard shouting. This was a typical piece of Michael manipulation and harassment, it appeared that one of the working girls had been moved, you see you don't ask for a new flat with these people, it just happens. The poor girl, one of the younger ones that I knew as Jasmine was dragged up the stairs with a hastily packed bag, and was put in a ground floor room a couple of doors down. The shouting wasn't coming from the girl, she knew better than argue but from the resident of the flat above. It was an old man that I recognised not because he was trouble or a face I had seen around much, in fact the only time I had seen him was at the residents meeting. Michael had picked him to show the others at the meeting what to expect. "Working girls work in shifts so there would be another one or two girls" sharing the room for business, in other words the poor residents of the house could now expect the coming and going of the girls' clients day and night, they would be finding used condoms dumped on the doorstep and their door bells pressed in error all night long.

A Life on the Lane

Once Jasmine was moved Michael and his bodyguard walked back down towards the play area and stopped, he placed both hands on the high chain link fence and laughed as he scanned the makeshift football pitch. His eyes eventually hit on the person he was looking for, me. This was going to serve as a message for Eric, he knew exactly how long it would take for me to get to Linda's place and let Eric know what had happened and what's more he didn't need to expend any energy in getting the message out. I almost felt guilty for doing his dirty work but I knew Eric should be told.

Linda came to the door when I got there, "Malcy what you doing here, it's Sunday morning", Linda was still in her best dress, she had been to church with her family, I knew that within a few minutes Eric would be off to the pub and I needed to speak with him. "Yeah sorry Lin but I need to see your dad, it's about umm …..The Stall." Lin looked sceptical, even though I was a trained liar Linda was different, lying convincingly to her was impossible. She took me up the stairs to the living room. Eric was just combing the brylcream into his hair, he turned and looked at the two of us in the door way. "Ere dad Malc says there's a problem with the stall", "yeah it's umm", I glanced at Linda and Eric got the message. "Linda nip in the kitchen for a minute this is boring market stuff and you know the tiddler gets embarrassed when he's cocked up". Linda left the room shutting the door behind her. Eric pulled his pocket watch out of his waistcoat pocket and said "Well tiddler there's a pint down the Pelican with my name on it, what's so important you feel the need to keep me from it?" I told Eric what had happened and he shrugged it off as a coincidence but he understood the message that Michael had sent and even though he didn't show it, he was aware of the implied threat. Eric left the house but instead of heading towards the Pelican he headed straight to Mr. Watkins house. This was exactly what Mr. Watkins had predicted in the meeting, it was as if Michael was working from a script, it was so predictable but no one expected it to start so soon.

I wandered back to the playground to collect my jacket, in all the excitement I had left it behind, it wasn't a problem all the lads Bobby, Freddy, Kit, Tony and the rest would make sure it was safe, it's not that it was worth anything but we didn't have much and what we did have we liked to keep hold of. What was important were the little bits and bobs in the pocket, a small key ring penknife from Woollies, about sixpence in pennies and the most silly thing of all a ring made from the bottle top from our school milk, the ring had been given to me by Linda one day after school, she told me it was our engagement ring, and that I had to keep it forever. Unknown to her I did keep it and would, in quiet times alone slip it on my finger and imagine that we were old enough to really be engaged, I would have been devastated had I lost it. I got my jacket and decided that if my prized possessions were to be safe and secure I should hide them, I had just the place. Off I ran down to St Luke's Mews where I climbed over the stacks of rubbish and found the loose brick in the back wall. This was my special hiding place, I told no one about it and as far as I knew there was no one else that would bother to get into such a filthy place just to find a loose brick. That was it I had deposited two pence of my money and the ring behind the brick and wedged it back, I scraped a hand full of dirt up and filled in the gap around the brick, job done now I could go off and find something to do.

A Life on the Lane

I walked around for about an hour looking for someone to tie up with but apart from a couple of the boys playing football it was dead and what's more it was starting to rain. Just as I was getting to the point when even I was going to go home I saw Linda leaving Sue's house, I shouted to her, I'd rather walk her home than see her walk down Powis Gardens alone. Linda's eyes lit up and we walked back to her house to go over the weekend's homework. I always managed to do the least I could and at the last moment, I knew my mum would ask after my supper if I had homework, that was my cue to get changed for bed and spend a little time in the bedroom doing maths or whatever and a lot of time reading comics. As I closed my eyes to sleep I couldn't help wondering what excitement tomorrow would bring and with thoughts of the day's happenings running through my mind I drifted off to sleep.

Monday morning began as any other, the walk to school along the lane past all the stalls with good morning after good morning all the way. I managed to gather so many different names along that few hundred yards, "morning Tiger", "morning short arse", "lookout the ankle snappers about", they were all said in good humour, you knew you were popular if you got so many different names but when I got to Eric's there was no "morning tiddler ere's ya lunch", there was no apple or orange tossed across the stall, Eric wasn't there. Paul was alone behind the jump, "where's the governor Paul not gone sick has he?" "No he was here to set up then said he had some business to sort out, but he wasn't himself" Paul replied, "oh never mind see you later". That was it time for school, I always managed to be the last in and the first out of the playground, I could time it to perfection without being late.

In class I was anxious to ask Linda if her Dad was OK, "well he was Ok last night, I didn't see him this morning." I let it slip from my mind, it was none of my business anyway but with all that was going on I had been a bit concerned.

School was the usual bore only interrupted by the mid morning clip around the ear from Mrs. Love and the flying blackboard eraser coming from the same hand in the afternoon, do you know what, I'm of the opinion that having a lady teacher was a right result, had that been a bloke that slung the eraser I would have been in accident and emergency as we speak.

I chose to walk home along the market and not with Linda like I usually did but I just wanted to see who was on the stall, "hello tiddler you lost your way?" Eric was back and seemed on top form, "hello Eric, no I just had enough of the girlie chat so left Linda to walk home with Sue, I missed out on my fruit this morning that Paul's a bit of a tight wad". I didn't really care about the apple I just wanted to see if Eric mentioned where he was for the morning shift. "Should've helped yourself tiddler - then Paul could have had some practice squashing your finger with the tealeaf stick". The tea leaf stick was a piece of round wood about the size of a baseball bat which was used to shall we say frighten off thieves and needless to say the rhyming slang for thief is, well I'm sure I don't need to spell it out. Eric turned to a lady waiting to be served and I knew it was conversation over, nothing else to say, so off I went.

Monday evening was going to be short, the rain had set in and it was girls' games round at Lin's. Sue and Lin were doing the dolly bit in the hall of Lin's house so I took my leave and wandered off to my house and a big pile of superman comics

A Life on the Lane

I'd got off Bobby. The winter was the best time to read the comics in my bedroom, I'd slip into bed and read by the light of a torch, my mum would moan like mad telling me I'd ruin my eyes but it was an escape. I was there in Metropolis watching Superman not in a grotty flat in Notting Hill; sometimes I just got completely lost in the stories and would fall asleep by the failing light of my torch. Mum would come in and search the bed for comics, turn off the torch, tuck me in and kiss me on the forehead, it's funny I never knew she did it until later in life, I didn't even wonder how the bedroom got sorted by the morning but it always did.

CHAPTER 4
LIFE WILL NEVER BE THE SAME

It was Wednesday morning and I had to walk to school in a real pea-souper one of those fogs that London used to get because of all the coal fires. The fog was a horrible grey yellow colour and so thick you could taste it, it was awful so I used to pull a scarf up around my face. It was a good job I knew where I was going, down Westbourne Park Road and turn left into Portobello Road and so on, "Morning Tiger" that was Albert the flower man, the warm glow of the lights on the stalls and the friendly voices of the stallholders made me feel safe, I could find my way to school now and know that everything was going to be alright. I got to Eric's and shouted "morning boss, you're not going to be able to see the punters coming today are you?" Eric just grunted and for the first time ever it was Paul that slung an apple to me, "go on get off to school Malc" he said, "Eric's got a sore throat and gabbing with you will only make it worse".

In class everything was as normal, Linda was at her desk when I walked in the classroom, Mrs. Love was tapping her hand with the twelve inch ruler and Freddy was about to sit down at the desk next to mine. Freddy lived in the flats opposite our flat, he was a good laugh always had something funny to say and could take a joke as well. I think he had it quite tough at home. There were 4 kids in his family, not that

A Life on the Lane

that was unusual most families were considerably larger than the modern norm of 2.4 children, some, especially the Irish kids had five, six or even more brothers and sisters. As I was saying Freddy had it a bit tough, even though he was only ten he was the oldest child so he was the one that had to look after the other kids, even at night if his parents were going out, and it was Freddy that was first up and had to get the others ready for school and then take them. As I said Freddy was a laugh and I never heard him moan about what he had to do for his brother and sisters, it made me realise how lucky I was, I was the youngster in my family.

Wednesday was going to be boring, the fog meant there was nothing to look out of the classroom window at, even the pigeons that roosted on the ledges alongside the windows had gone walkabout. I owe them pigeons a lot, because it was the pigeons that were amongst the more entertaining subjects in the University of Life, well can I just mention the birds and the bees? Those birds taught me all I know about the mating process, in the spring it was all there, the secrets of the mating season played out before our eyes, trouble was it didn't half give me a headache. Not what they were doing but from the slaps around the back of the head from Mrs. Love, still I've got a lot to thank those filthy flying rats for.

The day's schooling came to an end and I was gone, straight down the markets. I stopped off at the stall and helped Eric out trimming a few cauliflowers for him, "ere tiddler hang around and give Paul a hand for a bit, I've gotta pop down the road for a minute" said Eric and he was away.

"That's unusual" I said to Paul "what's unusual". "Well" I responded "Eric's gone in the bookies; he never goes in there during the week". Paul looked down towards the betting office then turned to me, " it's best you mind your own business Malc, Eric's got stuff on his mind and you sticking your nose in it won't best please him, if I were you I wouldn't mention the bookies to Eric or anyone else". That was well put I thought, in other words keep mum even with Linda.

Eric got back with a worried look on his face, Paul looked at me and said "go on Malc; go home this fog ain't going to clear so get back before it gets too dark". Ok I thought message understood and off I went. I hadn't got more than a couple of stalls up the road when I realised that I had left my school bag at the stall so I turned and headed back. Paul and Eric were talking so I ducked down and slid under the stall to grab my bag. I heard Eric telling Paul with a distinct tremble in his voice that he had lost a tenner on a horse, ten pounds which was a huge amount of money for someone like Eric. "It came second to a bloody nag called Tempus Fugit, 20 to 1 that came in at, what the bloody hell am I going to do now, and how can I tell the wife I've lost that sort of money on a horse". I grabbed my bag and slipped back out from under the stall, neither of them saw me and I rushed off home with Eric's words playing in my head over and over again. Tempus Fugit, I had no idea what it meant except that it had cost Eric a lot of money and probably a lot of pain, what trouble was he in that had made him gamble so much on a horse race after all the average wage for a full grown worker was only about fifteen quid a week?

I went home and went to my bedroom, "not having your supper tonight Malc"? "No I'm not hungry mum, I'm just going to do my homework then go to bed". My mum came in felt my forehead, "you coming down with something" she enquired. "No I just want to be left alone" I snapped,

26

A Life on the Lane

"sometimes I just need to be alone".   My mum said in her soothing voice "OK Malc, I'm going to cook your supper and if you want it later it will be there for you". About an hour later I came out of my room all I could think about was that horse and its name Tempus Fugit, it was going round and round in my head like a top, over and over I heard myself saying it to myself. "Mum what is Tempus Fugit?"   "Where did you get that from? It's Latin I think" she said, "something to do with time, time flies, yes that's it time flies".   That's typical I thought Eric's been stuffed by a horse that isn't even English but I had no idea where Latin was, anyway with that horse's name now translated I decided it was time to eat my supper, I knew we didn't have a lot so wasting the food we could only just afford was not really an option.

Thursday came around and the fog had lifted it was yet another day at school and I had decided to walk in with Linda, trouble was I was always "a just in time student" so I needed to run a bit to catch up with her before she got to the school gate because at that point it was girls and boys in separate parts of the school until we got into class. As I got to Powis Square I could see Linda at the other end of the road, she was walking with Sue and Sue's mum. Sue's mum was a diner lady at the school as was Linda's mum. Their mum's had been working together at the school for years so they knew each other really well and the girls would spend loads of time with each other playing dolls and girlie stuff like that. "Hello Mrs. W, you OK" I said when I caught up with them. "Hello Malc what are you doing walking this way to school today?"   "Oh I was just a bit late so didn't want to go down the Lane, you know me I'd end up rabbiting with someone down there and be late for school then I'd end up getting a clip round the ear from Mrs. Love, thing is I think she enjoys it too much, clipping me round the ear I mean". We walked on chatting but in the back of my mind I was still thinking about Eric, which was the real reason I didn't go past the stall this morning.

The day passed slowly and I'd managed to say to Linda that I was going to walk home with her after school, it made my day she was really pleased. Sue had to go to the eye hospital in the afternoon so Lin was planning on walking home alone. Thursday was a funny day because it was half day closing, my dad would always go to the pictures and Eric was at home or down the lock up doing some repairs to the hand barrows or stall, I usually walked down there just to see if I could help but today I wanted to stay with Lin.

Come the end of the day I tried to get out of school as soon as possible but that was a mistake, when I got down to the first landing Mrs. Love was on my case, "Malcolm come back here", I knew exactly what was wrong, I was running on the stairs, a crime that could result in being kept behind for a quarter of an hour, I didn't want to keep Lin waiting or knowing that she had walked home alone, there was only one thing for it, I had to crawl. "Sorry Mrs. Love I know I was being a bit quick but .... "But nothing" Mrs. Love interrupted, "you know the rules and you know what the punishment is, back up to the classroom". I was absolutely amazed when I got back to the classroom because within 2 minutes of sitting back at the desk Lin walked in, she too had been rushing to get out with the aim of being at the gate before me, as she walked in we looked at each other and the grins on our faces went from ear to ear.

After the fifteen minutes of sitting in silence we were told to go and this time walk down the stairs, we did and met at the

A Life on the Lane

gate and wandered off chatting and laughing as we went.

Within twenty minutes we had reached Lin's home and she asked if I wanted to come in for a while, I wasn't sure because as it was Thursday and that was half day closing, I was guessing there a chance Eric was there but before I had the opportunity to think I found myself saying "yes as long as your mum and dad don't mind". Lin pushed the front door and we were greeted by raised voices coming from the first floor landing. Outside the Browns living room door were what to Lin and I were the huge figures of three men, I knew immediately who it was. "Peter the Pole" and Michael had their backs to us and the third man was looking down the stairs towards the front door, Eric and Mrs. Brown were in the living room trying to keep them out. As the front door rattled against the inside wall of the hallway, Michael lunged at Eric and without thinking Lin rushed up the stairs screaming, Michael turned as she reached the landing and pushed Lin away. My heart stopped as she lost her footing, there was only one way to go and that was down. I had followed Lin into the hall and was by now standing at the bottom of the stairs and as I looked up Lin was on her way down bouncing off every other step on the way. Time slowed to the point where I saw every bump of her body and heard every whimper as she got closer, I even heard the sound of the radio coming from the Browns living room.

Lin came to rest at my feet and I knew she was in a bad way, just how bad I didn't yet understand, Eric and Mrs. Brown screamed in unison, piercing heart wrenching screams that I will hear for the rest of my life. I looked hard into Lin's eyes and I knew the vibrant smiling and happy Lin I knew was gone, at that point a single drop of blood ran down from her nose and settled on her top lip.

Mrs. Browns screams turned to sobs, I looked up the stairs and the three men were on their way down. Those monsters were grinning and at one point Michael actually laughed, when they got to the bottom of the flight of stairs they stepped over Lin without even looking at her, she was just a piece of discarded rubbish to them, what could I do, I was no match for them, they could just stroll out as if nothing had happened.

The Browns knelt by Lin still crying and saying her name over and over again, Eric was repeating they've hurt my little girl over £175, how could they, they're animals, sub human. Then the harsh reality dawned on all of us, Linda was dead, this precious life had been ended by a flick of a powerful arm, gone never to return, I would never hear her giggles or see her smiling face again. I just couldn't take it anymore and ran. I didn't touch the outside steps I leapt straight onto the pavement and smashed heavily into an old lady that was walking by. I don't know if I hurt her but just for a second it stunned me, then as I regained my senses I was off at full speed, I have no idea where I ran to I just ran.

It wasn't until much later in the evening when I started to think logically, I was sitting under the canal bridge at the top end of Ladbroke Grove, I had to think what to do, should I go home or even could I go home. I wasn't sure if those hoodlums would be waiting for me, were they as I sat there in the dark waiting outside my own home or were they finishing the job at Eric's home. Just then I heard the ringing of a police car's bell, it should have been of comfort to a small boy that was still terrified of what was going to happen but it wasn't and as the police car passed over the bridge above me

A Life on the Lane

all I could do was sit and sob.

It must have been about midnight when I heard voices and I looked around to see the beams from a pair of torches coming towards me, I was freezing, the temperature by the canal on that winter's night hadn't affected me until that minute, I immediately jumped to my feet which of course meant that I presented an unmistakable silhouette to whomever it was that was on the towpath. As I turned to run I heard them call "Malcolm, Malcolm it's alright we are the police, we've been looking for you. For a moment I stopped, were they really the police or Michael's heavies, I couldn't take a chance; I started to run again but was too close to the bank. I lost my footing and ended up in the murky waters of the Grand Union Canal, I have never been so cold in all my life and I struggled to draw a breath before I slipped below the water. It wasn't that I couldn't swim, one of my favourite pastimes was swimming at Silchester public baths, but that was different for a start the water was a bloody sight warmer and I had never been in the pool fully clothed including my school shoes. I managed to get to the surface for a brief moment and this time gulped as much air as a small boy could but as quickly as I went up I was on my way down again, I remember thinking this isn't the way it was supposed to end, both Lin and I dead within a few hours of each other, I knew we should never be separated but I didn't for one second think that meant we would be brought together in such tragic circumstances.

At that moment I heard a splash through the water and I made one last effort to fight my way back up to the surface, again I grabbed a lung full of air and this time I opened my eyes, there was a light shining straight at me but I was unable to stay on the surface long enough to see where the light was coming from. As I dropped for the third time I felt a strong hand on my collar and I was dragged to one side and up. Within a few seconds I was on the tow path coughing out what seemed like half the water in the canal whilst looking over me were the faces of two of the "Mets" finest. "You've led us a merry dance Malcolm", one of the coppers said "and my mate here hates going in the water, I practically had to throw him in to fish you out". He gave me his great coat to warm me up but it didn't work I was still freezing, the copper spoke gently to me   "don't worry son your safe now, we know what has happened and exactly what you've been through, now my mate Tom here is going to run up to the phone box and get you a lift home". His gentle but strong voice was putting me at ease and I just let it all go, I cried out loud, the tears rolled down my cheeks in floods but it was good, I needed to let it out.

While we sat there waiting for a police car to arrive the most stupid things passed through my mind, "I need to confess sir" I blurted out to the copper. He looked down at me in amazement, "look son you don't need to say anything yet, its best you sleep on it tonight". "No" I insisted   "I need to tell you, back in the summer we took a pram so that we could put the wheels on a soap box cart and I threw the pram bit in the canal just about here. I'm sorry it was a stupid thing to do, I only thought about it when I was bobbing up and down in the water".   The copper looked at me and smiled, "it's all right we won't be pressing charges anyway we're the only ones that know and I'm not going to tell anyone. Let's forget about it "yeah"! Stupid I know but I felt a bit better. It didn't seem long before we heard footsteps and the other "Bobby" came in sight "the area car's here to take Malcolm home he'll

A Life on the Lane

be tucked up in bed in no time".

It wasn't the first time that I had been taken home by the police but this time I wasn't going to get a slap from my dad, as the policeman rang the door bell I got a feeling of relief, probably a similar feeling as my parents got when they opened the door to see their bedraggled son flanked by two bloody great Coppers. My mum answered the door and I don't know how she didn't break my back she hugged me so hard, but it felt good, at the top of the stairs my dad looked down at the gathering below and in a shaky voice he called out my name, I don't know if he wanted confirmation it was me, or just needed to attract my attention, my attention he got and I broke away and walked steadily up the stairs. My dad was never an emotional man, I could count the number times he cuddled me on the fingers of one hand but this time he really meant it, he didn't mince his words, " Eric told us what happened, they won't get away with it, we are all going to make sure of that".

The police came in and while getting ready for a hot bath I heard them say that someone would come round to see me tomorrow. Mum started to run the water and it drowned out the rest of the conversation. I soaked in the bath until the police left, they called in just to reassure me all would be OK but all I wanted to do at that point was go to bed, as all children I felt safer under my covers. Sleep came on me almost instantly and it was a relief not to dream, it was just black, still, and resting.

When the morning came I got up and started to get ready for school, I took a clean shirt, pants and socks from the drawer and looked for a pair of trousers in the wardrobe but there wasn't any, I only had one pair of school trousers and they were wet. This minor problem was more than I could take, I just screamed and threw everything to the floor; mum came in and pulled me to her. I'd had a lot of words spoken in my ears over the last half a day, but mum knew what to say. As she cuddled me she just told me to let it all out, say what I had to say, she knew I wanted to tell someone and she was the best person to confide in. I blurted it all out, sometimes I cried, sometimes I shouted but I told all, it brought a tear to my mum's eye, she was well aware of how I felt about Lin, she herself had looked on Lin as a second daughter, but what I didn't expect to see was dad in the doorway, tears falling like rain, he looked me in the eyes and turned away.

I didn't go to school that day, I waited until the police came to take a statement, again I had to go over all that had happened, I had to tell them how Lin had tumbled down the stairs and I described every bump and contact that her head had made as she fell. I told how Michael had laughed and stepped over Lin but the one thing I couldn't tell them was that I actually saw Michael push Linda intentionally down the stairs. I didn't understand it was almost like they didn't want him to be the one that had taken Lin from me, from her family and from all the people that loved her. Time and again they asked me did I see Michael push her and time and again I couldn't say I saw the contact just a body movement. I had let her down by not stopping what had happened and now I was letting everyone down because I couldn't get that animal locked up where he belonged.

I stayed off school for a fortnight, it was too much to sit in class with an empty desk to the side of me, to me it seemed impossible to ever go back, I still wanted to run away but I knew that the support from my family was the only thing that

A Life on the Lane

was getting me through this and anyway I had to be at Lin's funeral. When I went back to school it was awful, in class I was distant and empty, I didn't dare to turn and look at Lin's desk and during playtime and lunch I just sat under the covered area. I would sit there thinking of what the future was going to be; sometimes I could feel the other kids and even the teachers watching me.

It was Mrs. Love that eventually came to me and spoke about what had happened, without saying so much she made it clear she was aware of how I felt about being in the classroom, "I'm sorry to do it at a time like this" she told me, "but it's time to move the pupils around, to bring the students that are good at some subjects to the front of the class where they can be better involved in the lesson". I hardly acknowledged her so she continued "when we go back after lunch you will be moving to the second row of desks along with Keith. You need to empty your effects from your desk and take the desk that has your name on it" with that she turned and left the playground. Not for one second did she hesitate or turn to look to see if I was watching. You hard cow I thought but she knew exactly what she was doing, this reshuffle was for me but I mustn't think that. When I and the other kids took up our new desks it all became clear, Lin's empty desk wasn't Lin's anymore and secondly because I had been moved forward it wasn't in my eye line anymore.

After all the investigations and post mortem, Lin's body was finally released for burial after five weeks, it seems daft but it meant that at last we could move on a bit, at last I could stop thinking about her laying somewhere alone and cold. In my few years on earth I hadn't really thought about death or what happens to people when they die, the closest I had come to death was when a couple of us found a foetus in the grounds of All Saints Church. It was tiny only about four inches long, at first we thought it was a dead bird but closer inspection proved that wrong. We used to play in the grounds of the church and were often chased off by the priest but on this occasion we needed to find him. I went to the rectory and just grabbed him by the arm, "we've found a body I blurted out, and you have to come". The priest followed as I half walked and half ran round to the side of the church, sure enough there it was the body of a tiny human being and I saw a look in the eye of the priest which showed why he was what he was. I saw a man that had seen this sort of thing before, his parish was made up of the poor, prostitutes and uneducated people that would find looking after this child impossible. Was it the result of a miscarriage or a self induced abortion we will never know but in the end the mother tried to give her off spring the best funeral she could, she must have felt that she should lay the child to rest in a church rather than dispose of it in some other unmentionable manner.

The priest made us leave so I have no idea what happened to that baby but I'm sure it was given a Christian send off in some way, as I said I am sure this wasn't the first time the priest had faced this type of situation and that he would do all that was right for this little soul. I think that is why I was grateful that Lin would be laid to rest now, I knew that I would not forget her or what had happened but it was the first of many steps I would need to face before I could really come to terms with what had happened.

It was Friday morning and we all got up early, for once without any complaint, today was to be Lin's funeral. My dad

A Life on the Lane

had washed our car, a 1952 Triumph Mayflower, we hadn't had it long and it stood out, parked outside on All Saints Road because in those days in that area few people had cars. At 11am we all walked to Eric's home, it was a walk I had taken hundreds of times but today my head was a mile away, I simply wasn't there in mind just body.

I sat in Eric's living room while we waited for the hearse to arrive, I have no idea if it was five minutes or five hours, time had become elastic sometimes it was stretched out so that days seemed like months, and other times compressed so that I had no idea whether it was morning or night.

When it was nearly time to leave dad went and got the car, I remember thinking I'm going to be miles behind Lin there will be all the funeral cars in front. I don't know how long it took to get to Surrey but I remember the cortege sweeping in through the wrought iron gates of the cemetery.

The cemetery was miles away from Notting Hill in Mortlake which is by the Thames, I thought Lin would like that, it's by the river and almost, or so I thought, in the country, without thinking I said out loud "Yeah" she'll be comfortable here". "What's that son" my dad said, I'd only mumbled so he didn't hear my words, "nothing dad just thinking out loud". I was in my own way making sure that this place was suitable for her and it was a good job it was. In my state of mind if I had felt it wasn't up to scratch I would have kicked off.

We all went in the chapel and I really was pleased to see the priest from All Saints was taking the service, again I looked deep into his eyes which he must have felt because he looked straight back at me with a look of recognition. As we looked at each other he mouthed a blessing which although I didn't understand gave me strength. I looked at the coffin standing on a trestle like contraption in the aisle and I thought, it's tiny she can't possibly be in there, but in reality I knew she was, she was in there at rest, peaceful, still and above any kind of pain or hurt.

I don't really remember anymore about the service or the funeral and as we stood there in the cold I was oblivious to the proceedings. I was standing near Eric and at one point I felt him put his hand on my shoulder, which seemed ironic but welcome and for the first time in weeks I cried.

After Lin was buried Eric put his arm around me and started to lead me away, I hesitated looked around and again mumbled "Linda will be happy with this place", Eric responded with a hug and reassuring words, "she will, it's quiet, she liked being quiet, come on, enough tears lets go home". It says a lot for Eric that he still had time for me even at his daughter's funeral.

As time went on I became more and more rebellious, more aggressive and more distant from my family and friends, I was ignoring my schoolwork and even stopped going to Eric's stall on a Saturday. I don't know if I even spoke to Eric for weeks, maybe months, which was even pointed out to me by Mrs. Brown. Jean, as I had taken to calling Mrs. Brown cornered me one day at the play area and in no uncertain terms told me that by ignoring Eric I was hurting him and hurting him hard, he had done nothing to hurt me and in fact had treated me like a son. All of this was true but I just didn't care, I was still hurting and being kind or nice to Eric or anyone else would not relieve my pain, just one thing would help and that was to have Lin back but of course we all knew that was impossible.

A Life on the Lane

The months went by and soon it would be the summer holidays, it meant six weeks of not being cooped up in a classroom but it also meant that Michael would be on trial. I know it sounds like I wanted revenge on him and maybe I did, maybe I was hoping he would hang or die in prison which to me seemed somewhat appropriate. I was in my juvenile hate filled way just waiting to hear that they or at least Michael would be doing the "Tyburn dance", dangling at the end of the hangman's rope. Albert Pierpoint was the official executioner but in my mind he was too good at his job, from what I had heard he would dispatch them quickly and cleanly, that's not the way I wanted to hear that Michael had departed this world.

It was a funny summer break because I still avoided the market, my life during school holidays up until that point had revolved around market life, I remember on numerous occasions Eric telling me to "bugger off and enjoy yourself with your mates, it's coming to something when you have to tell a kid to go and get into some mischief", but I just loved being there.

Of course I did miss the few bob I picked up doing bits and bobs but I soon worked my way around that, I'm not particularly proud of it but over the 6 weeks I became a dab hand at shoplifting. I just seemed to fall in with the wrong crowd, I wasn't mucking about with Bobby or Freddy this holiday, in fact I actively avoided all my mates, even Sue was shunned in favour of some kids from Moorhouse Road.

Towards the end of the holiday we ventured down Portobello Road, not to see Eric or anyone else but to visit Woolworths, "Woollies" as we knew it was easy pickings for kids with a sticky hand.

About 10 of us went into "Woollies", its better doing it in numbers because they can't watch all of you and there's less chance of getting caught. First stop was the counter that had penknives and stuff, I don't know why young boys have a fascination with knives but we all did. I managed to pocket a small knife with a bottle opener, which was easy it fitted neatly in the palm of my hand before deftly slipping it into the pocket of my jeans. Next was the sweet counter, small twopenny bars of Cadburys were the pick of the day, not because that was my favourite but because again they were small enough to palm and were close to the front of the counter. The more expensive sweets like Mars bars and larger bars of chocolate were at the back of the counter and were actually out of reach for someone that was only three feet and a fag paper tall. After the sweets I moved onto the toy counter which is where it all went wrong. I still don't know why but I wanted the Airfix kit of a Spitfire, so went directly for it, but it was my single minded determination to have it that was to be my downfall. I had simply made a beeline for that Spitfire, I didn't look around or listen to what was going on and without a second thought slid the kit off of its hook and put it under my sloppy Joe shirt. The next thing I knew was the other kids were shouting run and without thinking I was on my toes. I headed straight for the doors not worrying who or what was in the way, I remember bouncing off a big bloke in one of the aisles and hitting a kid about my age so hard he went down on the floor leaving his mother to shout out and try to clump me as I went by, but I was there, I had made it to the doors and once out in the Lane I knew I could get away from any chasing shop staff.

As I legged it along the market I didn't realise where I was, I was rapidly closing on Eric's stall and luckily the bloke that

A Life on the Lane

was chasing was dropping back, but my relief at outpacing my chaser was short lived. Eric had seen what was coming towards him and had stepped round to the front of his stall, of all the people to stop my escape in its tracks I would have put Eric behind Sherlock Holmes and Attila the Hun, but Eric it was. First off I thought he hadn't recognised me but without a second's delay he looked at me and almost in tears he asked in his quietest tones "what are you becoming Malc, what do you think you are up to, this just isn't you, running wild." Just then the manager from "Woollies" arrived and took hold of me by the collar, "thanks mate this little tearaway, visited almost every counter in the shop before we tried to collar him, I don't know how he thought he was going to get away with it, especially as he was so blatant, he didn't even look around him at the toy counter, anyway thanks mate, I was just about to give up when you caught him". Eric didn't respond and I couldn't look at him as I was marched back to the shop.

When we got back to "Woollies" I was led through the shop to the Manager's office where I was sat on a chair to await the arrival of the police. To my surprise I was the only one there; all the other kids had got away by the look of it. I was sitting in that office for about fifteen or twenty minutes with a member of the staff watching over me. He was a bloke about twenty-ish, he stood in front of the door but he looked so out of place and on edge, he obviously didn't like what he was doing. "What's up with you mate" I enquired "you could let me go you know, I won't do it again, it was just a stupid game that got out of hand". He looked at me with a knowing look and for the first time spoke. "And why would I let you go, for a start I'd lose my job and secondly I know your sort, come tomorrow you'll be out at the shops doing it all over again", and with that the door opened the Manager came in followed closely behind by a six foot copper. "Off you go Simon get back to work now and keep your eyes open for any of this little hooligan's friends" the Manager growled. I looked up at the policeman and my heart sank, of all the coppers around the area it had to be him, the one policeman I very nearly owed my life to. As I stared at him I could see the look of recognition "hello Malc what you been up to then?" I couldn't answer, my throat became dry and I couldn't swallow, standing there in front of me was the copper that had found me under the canal bridge the night Linda had died, the copper that had comforted and warmed me, had listened to my confession and had wiped away my tears, but this time it was different, you see I had somehow lost much of my emotional self, I didn't cry now in fact I didn't smile, laugh or do most things kids of my age do, I had become cold and heartless.

The copper looked at the shop manager and asked to have a word with him outside before he was to take me away, they left the office and again the door was closed, I wasn't very keen at being closed in but something told me to take a deep breath and wait. I wasn't more than a few minutes when the door opened again and the policeman came in alone, he took me by the collar but this was different to the way the manager had held me, "come on Malc, let's take you home again, I think we need to have a chat" he said.

We walked off towards my home, past Eric's stall but I just didn't look, I couldn't understand why he had caught me and then handed me over to the shop manager, it didn't seem right to me. As we walked the copper talked to me, " My names PC Jones, Richard Jones, we need to talk Malc, I had a

A Life on the Lane

bit of a job persuading the manager not to press charges, he wanted you banged up but I convinced him you were worth another chance, I need you to promise me you won't let me down". That was an easy get out for me, a simple promise and I was off, scot free, easy, job done I thought. "Yeah I promise" I responded but it must have sounded hollow to PC Jones, "well it's not quite that simple" he announced, "because I'm going to take you home and explain to your mum what you've been up to, so you still have her to answer to and your dad when he gets home". Now then I thought my dad was more of a problem.

When we got back to my place Richard rang the door bell and waited, not in, I thought but my relief was short lived because the door opened and my mum was standing there, "I'm sorry to bother you but we need to have a chat about Malc, he's been in a bit of trouble, nothing too serious but we need to nip it in the bud". It was the same old story I was sent to my room while mum and the copper had a chat. It must have been about half an hour when I heard the front door close and my mum clomping back up the stairs and across the hall towards my bedroom. I had heard her steps a million times before but this time there was a determination in them, she was coming and I had a feeling that what was coming was going to hurt, I didn't have to wait long. The bedroom door flew open and mum stood there with fire in her eyes, the comic I was reading was ripped from my hands and I thought "this is not good" with an almost seamless movement her hand whistled towards my head, she had never before hit me around the head, I knew that this was a heartfelt punishment. "What do you think you are up to, you've taken to ignoring your friends, Freddy was almost in tears the other day because you haven't seen him during the summer break and even Sue's mum says you've ignored her and Sue and now you've been out shoplifting. You are letting everyone down, PC Richard has had to almost beg the manager at "Woollies" not to press charges and even Eric thinks you have lost it Malc. If you're wondering how I know about Eric it's because he came here after he had handed you over to the shopkeeper. That man is going out of his mind because of you, he did nothing to hurt you and you have been treating him like dirt, why Malc why?" That was it I flipped "it's because of Eric that Lin's dead, he gambled money away that he owed "Peter the Pole" and that's why Michael killed Lin, it's all Eric's fault". My mum was speechless I had worked this all out myself and had kept it a secret from everyone until now.

What I had said shocked mum and without another word she turned and left the room closing the door behind her. I guessed that meant I had to stay in my room which was hardly a punishment, I only enjoyed my own company these days and would immerse myself in the comics that I kept in a box by the bed. I didn't cry even though the slap I had got from mum had been a real screamer, it's not that I didn't want to cry it's just that after all the pain I had been through and all the tears I had cried there was nothing left.

That was it really for the summer, six weeks wasted, spent moping around or getting in trouble, maybe this was the passage into adulthood because after the holiday I was going to be starting a new school. I was so relieved because I wouldn't be sitting in the classroom where Lin had been so happy and I had spent so much time by her side, I wanted to get away and start a new era in new surroundings. It was decided for me, that I should go to a school outside of the

A Life on the Lane

area even though it meant a trek to Shepherd's Bush every day. My parents were relaxed about the whole thing too because almost everyone else in the area were going to local schools and I wouldn't be mixing with the local hooligans that they thought had been leading me astray. How wrong could they be? I didn't need any help I was more than capable of wreaking havoc all by myself if I wanted. I had always been a strong person but up until now had channelled my strength in to the decent things in life; from now on it was going to be different.

CHAPTER 5
NOT A GOOD START

For anyone the first day at a new school is intimidating but for a maladjusted and angry eleven year old it was going to be a challenge. It was going to be a challenge seeing how far I could push the new teachers and if that went well how far I could push the system. I was determined to make myself a nuisance, someone that the teachers would remember for a long time, of course there was always the possibility that they would simply expel me which made me wonder, how many times you can be expelled before they give up and leave you alone to just read comics at home in your bedroom.

The big day came and Mum looked so proud, I had the new uniform with a crispy white shirt, neatly pressed trousers, nice clean shoes and even a tie, "how long is this lot going to last Malc"? Mum enquired. It's not that I wrecked my clothes intentionally it just sort of happened all by itself, some people are money magnets and some girl magnets but me I was a dirt magnet. If I put on new clothes you could guarantee that within ten yards of home they would be filthy and usually covered in things that don't warrant thinking about. So that was it a peck on the cheek and a wave goodbye and off on the number 7 bus and the new era was off to a great start. I had one shilling and eight pence for the day but before I even started out I had

A Life on the Lane

worked out the fiddles. If I just paid a twopenny fare each way on the bus instead of fourpence I would have enough left for a threepenny loose and a penny book match, "yes" I had started smoking and certain shops in the area would sell kids loose cigarettes. It was almost accepted that at some point everyone would start to smoke so for the shopkeepers if it was a few years ahead of schedule, what the heck.

"Twopenny half please" I asked the clippy and she spun the ticket machine and handed me the ticket, "that only gets you to North Pole Road son and your badge tells me you want to go to Du Cane Road, so I'll be keeping an eye on you." True to her word when we got to the scrubs she came back up stairs to turf me off the bus, I didn't mind the walk but the other kids on the bus had a good old laugh at my expense. This however was a good start for me because needless to say on my first day at school I was late, not just a little late but so late that all the new kids with exception of yours truly had met their new form teachers and been marched off to their classrooms. Where the bloody hell do I go, I wandered around the corridors looking in classrooms but not knowing anyone how would I know which was mine? My wanderings were ended by the bellowing of a master wearing a mortarboard and gown, "you boy, why are you not in your class?" It probably wasn't the most intelligent thing to do but I burst out laughing, I had only seen teachers dressed like that at the pictures, in films like St Trinian's. It was like a red rag to the bull the teachers face contorted with rage. "I'll ask you again, why are you not in your class" but this time he was inches from my face and so loud that it made my ears ache. I decided it would be prudent not to anger this man any further and answered in a confident but not so loud manner. "I'm new and ain't got the faintest idea where my class is mate".

"MATE you call me MATE" His face was now glowing red and I thought he was going to have a heart attack, "I should take it easy gov, you won't last long if you keep getting excited like that" I quipped. Quick as a flash he had hold of my ear and was marching me down the corridor, I didn't know where I was going but I knew if I didn't move at the same pace as the teacher I would lose my facial symmetry, even I felt that going along with him was far less painful than having my left ear torn off.

I was finally released at what I later found out to be the school secretary's office, I also found out that the master in the gown was in fact the deputy head, "what's you name boy and from now on you address me as Sir" he growled. "Malcolm Williams" I chirped "but everyone calls me Malc, I prefer that".   Mr. Clifford looked down his nose at the cheeky lad standing in front of him, the boy that had the bare faced cheek to call the Deputy Head mate was now telling him that he should be addressed as Malc. "You will from now until the time you either leave or are expelled be known as Williams, and my guess is it will probably be the latter".   The secretary flicked through her lists of new boys and found the required information "1A2 Mr. Clifford". "What 1A2 you are in the top stream Williams, why on earth are you in the top stream, you're too stupid to be in the top stream there must be some kind of mistake, oh never mind I'll sort it out later, let's get you in to a class any class before I lose my cool". Cool I thought, I don't think so Mr. Clifford, but I kept that to myself, I still wanted to keep both ears on the side of my head.

I finally got to my class and was given a desk right in the front row directly in front of the teacher, great I thought there will be

A Life on the Lane

no hiding in here, everything I get up to will be in full view of him, abso-bloody-lutely great. Well this is a right place I thought, it was my first day and it seemed that Mr. Clifford had given my rap sheet to every master in the school, the form master was sticking to me like glue and the master in the playground at break was watching me so intently his eyes seemed to be burning into me, then there was lunchtime, even the dinner ladies were on my case, I just didn't know how long I could take this without exploding.

School was school and I grew to understand quickly that I wasn't going to change it. I simply got on with it as best I could. For me there was a more pressing issue to look forward to, the trial of those responsible for taking Lin's life away. Those low life sub humans were going to be in court by the end of October and not before time. I had been called to the Police station on a number of occasions to give a statement, to go over all the minutia of that dreadful day. The smallest detail was captured again and again, I hated it, reliving the worst moments of my life for those that had decided it was necessary.

In those first few months at Christopher Wren School I lost count how many times I was put on detention and how many letters were sent to my parents, I was pushing the system and it wasn't budging. I did however make some good friends, friends that would stand by me even when sometimes I wasn't particularly nice to them. Jack was one of them, he was a good mate, we got on well from day one and we stuck together through whatever was thrown at us. Jack was the only reason I stayed at school, if it wasn't for him I simply would not have kept going there. I was well aware that his parents didn't like me, they thought I was leading him astray and well to be honest

49

I probably was, I am sure if we hadn't become mates he would do well at Wren but with me around his outlook wasn't too bright, I taught him to steal, bunk off school, swear and anything else that was against the rules, in fact we had an absolute whale of a time.

The weeks went by and the trial was getting closer, it wasn't that I was going to the trial, there was no such thing as video links in those days, my evidence would be read out for me. I knew that when it came to it my statement would be read out by a court official, it would be in mono tones with no feelings, no fear and no pauses to wipe away a tear, emotionless but how could it be any different. There was no way that anyone could do justice to my words, how could they, the reader would not have the emotional involvement that I had, the years of knowing such a wonderful person and then seeing her life snatched away in a few heartbeats.

October came and my head was exploding, I lived every moment of Linda's fall, I heard every word uttered by Eric and Jean and every whimper as she fell down the stairs over and over and over but I wasn't in court, I wasn't allowed, and what's more I didn't want to be. Even when I got home which was often late because of detentions or just running the streets I would hear the voices of Michael and Peter in my head and even though the Browns told my parents how the trial was going I never asked. My lack of success in blotting out what had happened was almost as consistent as Eric and Jean's attendance at the Old Bailey, they of course were not allowed into the courtroom until after they had given their evidence but they had enough contacts to be kept informed.

The case went on for three and a half weeks and what

A Life on the Lane

happened was a wake-up call for everyone in Notting Hill, not just the unlucky tenants of Peter, not just the working girls and not just the poor that they lent money to, but every single human being in the area. I don't know if they had got to the jury or the judge or what but those men had got away with it, there was no murder charge, no manslaughter not even an assault charge for what they did and they would be walking the streets free men knowing they got off with it. Everybody would now be fair game for them because now they had a belief that they were above the law, and to all of us it seemed they were. I went over what I was going to do to them every night as I lay awake in bed but I knew deep down that I was no match for them …. Yet, make no mistake one day I would make amends for not protecting Lin and for not being able to get her the justice I knew I owed her.

With the trial over I knew I had no trust in or respect for the law I seemed to have been given carte blanche to behave as I wanted, school was a long way down my list of must do things but I carried on going so that I could keep in with Jack and a couple of other lads there. I would roll in at what time it suited me and would bunk off if I got bored, I even blackmailed Jack telling him he wasn't much of a mate if he'd wanted to be in class rather than out tea leafing with me, but I didn't care. I pushed my mates to the limit of their friendship and beyond but incredibly they seemed to keep their faith in me, why though is a complete mystery to me but I learned a long time ago not to look a gift horse in the mouth.

November was a good month because no sooner were "Peter the Pole" and Michael laying down the law on the streets than Peter up and died, I would like to think that there had been some divine intervention or something but without the hand of a higher being this had to be put down to bad luck. I just thought that had he gone down his incarceration would have been short lived and had he got the death penalty he would not have been around long enough to see his appeal, all I thought was "so what, good riddance to bad rubbish" however the main perpetrator Michael was still around the neighbourhood, a visible memory of all that had happened, and reminders of my memories certainly were not needed.

The weeks turned into months and as they passed I knew it would soon be the summer break, the streets would be ours, we could run riot and because the schools were closed and there were enough young people around to make things interesting.   Our favourite pastime was buying a red rover ticket which gave us unlimited travel on the London bus network; this meant we could travel out to Epping in the east, Heathrow in the West, Croydon in the south and Watford in the North which was a big area to lose ourselves in. There were so many high streets to go stealing in and the escape route was the next bus to come along. We all knew it was only a matter of time before we got caught but that was a bridge to cross when we got to it.

Somehow summer came and went and I was still at large, my parents had started to lose patience with me, teachers seemed to be pleased if I bunked off and even my mates were getting fed up with my behaviour but even this I could take but through it all my mate Jack stayed loyal, he took all the crap I threw at him and was always the first one to stick up for me, even though I was probably ruining his future, if he carried on hanging out with me I doubt he would get any qualifications and

A Life on the Lane

his job prospects would diminish as a result. Never mind I thought it's his choice and anyway we would both be in the same boat, so what the hell.

School put up with me as the months turned to years and I knew that I could leave at fifteen to make my way in the big wide world but I needed to prepare myself, and Portobello Road was again becoming particularly important in my world. I was starting to frequent a different part of Portobello Road, it wasn't the fruit and veg market now because this was the swinging sixties. Things were happening further up the lane, there were hippies on the market now and if there were hippies there were drugs. I was progressing from tobacco to marijuana and if I wanted the dope I had to get the money to pay for it, which meant more thieving. I was getting good at stealing, in fact I would say I was the best in the area, I would steal clothes, shoes, handbags and just about anything that wasn't screwed down. Saturdays became the day for going to the antique part of Portobello Road because antiques meant tourists and tourists meant fat wallets and purses. These stupid tourists were so engrossed in antiques that they would put wallets down on market stalls while they looked at stuff, the women would walk around with handbags open and purses on display, it was so easy and so lucrative that I could make enough money on a Saturday to be stoned right through the week, and it was of course Jack that was there beside me in all of this.

We both knew that the bubble would burst soon and sure enough one Saturday when I was approaching fourteen it happened. Jack and I were watching a couple of Yanks, a man and woman around their thirties, they caught our eye because he had what looked like an expensive camera and was snapping away at everything. His wife was following behind with a large shoulder bag slung slightly backwards. I had seen the bloke on two occasions put his camera down while he looked at goods on a stall and once watched his wife pay for something from a fat purse taken from the now open shoulder bag.

Jack and I would work as a pair, he would stay pavement side of the stalls and I would follow the mark, that's the person we planned to rob, on the road side of the stall. Jack's job was to distract the mark, usually by engaging them in some kind of conversation while I robbed them. We were good at it to the point where I would say we were proud of how good we were and because of it I think I was getting too cocky. Sure enough the pair stopped at a stall and he put his camera down on the edge of the stall while he looked at some silver item, I winked at Jack to let him know I was going to go for it, and he started his routine. "Hello Gov" he started "you yanks then" he enquired "sure am" the bloke responded "oh yeah what bit?" That was it Jack had drawn his attention away from the camera, it was mine, I put my jacket down over it and looked around. I couldn't believe my luck the woman had pushed her bag backwards so it was almost behind her and her purse was in full view. I just couldn't resist it, I was good enough to get both, the dip in to her bag was a doddle then turn pick up my jacket and disappear into the crowds. It took just a couple of seconds, Jack was in full flow and the pair were so taken with him they saw nothing that was going on around them. I turned picked up my jacket with the camera under it and headed off.

I hadn't gone more than ten yards when my collar was grabbed by a big bloke, I hadn't seen him, but he had spotted me and he knew exactly what I was up to. I couldn't believe it I had fallen

A Life on the Lane

for a bloody sting, they weren't Yanks, they weren't even tourists they were the old bill, plain clothed police and I hadn't spotted them, no wonder it was so easy they were setting themselves up to be robbed.

I was carted off to Notting Hill Police station in a black Maria, I didn't know if they had got Jack but I was guessing he'd done a runner and got away, how wrong could I be. While I was being questioned by the custody Sergeant the male fake tourist came in clutching the collar of a now tearful Jack, I knew why he was in tears, he knew what to expect when his father was called into collect him. We went through all the rigmarole that comes with being arrested, the fingerprints, and the searches the sitting around in a cell waiting to find out if we would be charged. It wasn't new for me I had been through most of this before but Jack was a first timer, I could hear him sobbing in the next cell waiting for the inevitable, yes inevitable. It wasn't a case of if he got some sort of punishment just what the punishment would be and from whom, was it going to be the court or his dad. As I sat in the cell listening to Jack I started to get edgy, I don't know if I caught it from Jack or the realisation that for once I wasn't sitting in the headmaster's office or waiting for the local Bobby to give me an ear bashing for being a tearaway on the streets, this time I was looking at going to court and possibly being sent to a juvenile detention centre. I thought I was tough but sitting alone with all the thoughts going through my mind convinced me I wasn't that hard after all.

After an hour or so I heard footsteps heading down the corridor towards the cells, another poor bugger I thought but it wasn't it was two police officers coming to collect Jack and me for charging. It's funny but the sound those locks make is the same whether you are being locked in or let out, especially when you are going up to be charged. "Come on Malcolm, time to go up to see the desk Sergeant", as I left the cell I turned to see Jack emerging from the next cell. Jack looked terrible; his eyes were so red from the crying that he looked like he had been ten rounds with Billy Walker. For the first time in a long time I actually felt guilty about the way I was behaving, I had led Jack into this and something inside said that I must try to get him out of it and cut him adrift.

When we got up to the desk the Sergeant looked us up and down, wrote a few words on the pad in front of him and in the sternest voice I had ever heard asked if we had anything to say. That was it Jack was off crying again, "yeah I have" I piped up, "now is your chance, tell us why you are here looking at theft charges and not doing the things that normal kids of your age are doing". I looked down to the floor he had really taken the wind out of my sails. "Well come on lad let's hear it". I looked round at Jack then to the Sergeant, "it ain't Jacks fault he didn't have anything to do with all this, it was my fault, Jack was just chatting to the tourists and maybe tap them up for a few coppers by giving them a hard luck story, but I saw the camera and stuff and just went for it". The Sergeant again looked at the pair of us, looking deep into our eyes, " they say the eyes are the windows to the soul" he said "and I can see by those of your friend Malcolm that he has been led into this situation by someone that is manipulative and selfish, but...." he paused and stared at me, "you know that he is in as much trouble as you, you should be aware that he is guilty by association, it's simple and clear cut". Jack was still crying but now he was getting louder and more hysterical. Once again the Sergeant spoke in that stern and commanding voice "however that would be the

A Life on the Lane

view of the juvenile court who up until this point know nothing of this case, so Malcolm let me ask you, was it you alone that decided to steal from the officers in Portobello Road and as such take full responsibility for the crime?". I gulped deep I just never looked at it that way but I knew I could repay some of Jacks loyalty by getting him off the hook for this one, I looked at Jack and blurted it out, "yeah it was all my idea as I said Jack was just being a cheeky kid I was the one that took it too far and tried to nick the stuff off 'em".

The Sergeant picked up his pen and put a long line through one of the rap sheets in front of him, "is Jack's father in the reception constable?" "Yes sir he's been waiting for some time". The Sergeant turned his attention to Jack, "Jack from what I can see of you, you are a clever boy that has been somewhat led astray by a strong willed friend that you may want to decide is not as much of a friend as you thought. Chances are that if you continue to follow his lead you will end up before me again and next time I will not be in such a good mood. This time you have been lucky and will be sent home with your father with no charge against you, it will be him that you need to answer to now. Constable take Jack to clean his face up and you Malcolm you wait here while I go to see Jack's father, then we will be dealing with you". Jack and the constable left the custody suite as did the Sergeant, it was just me and the other constable standing there, waiting for what-ever was going to happen next.

"Hello Malc" I froze, that was a voice I knew but I didn't know anyone else was in the room, "looks like you've really done it this time, the Sergeant reckons your going down, but it had to happen sooner or later didn't it?" A tear rolled down my cheek but I managed to wipe it away before anyone saw it, "well Malc anything to say?" I turned to face this disembodied voice "PC Jones" I was still holding back a tear or two. "What's going to happen am I going to a detention centre?" "Looks like it Malc, the Sergeant doesn't put up with kids that are out of hand and getting themselves in trouble all the time, from what I hear you are going to be taking the rap for you and your mate, there's not a lot I can do to help you this time, trouble is the last time you got caught 'tea leafing' you made me a promise not to get into trouble again but here we are, causing problems again." PC Jones's voice got louder "why did I waste my time before, you are not worth it, you think the world owes you but believe me the world has no debts, when it comes to life it's you that has to do the paying back just to be allowed to remain in civilised society". I hadn't noticed the other constable leave the room but it was just me and Richard in there, he calmed down a bit and looked hard at me, his voice softened "I really felt you could do something with your life Malc but you have proved me wrong so far, do you think you deserve another chance?". There was a silent pause; I simply had no answer for him. "Come on Malc let me help you and try to help yourself", tears began to well up in my eyes but I didn't actually cry. This however was enough for PC Richard, he saw this and he knew there was still a chance for me. "You've really let me and your family down Malc but unlike you I'm not a quitter, I think there is still some of the old Malcolm in there and I want to set that old Malcolm free, it's for that reason I'm going to try to help just once more but don't promise me you are going to change because you've done that before and here we are again". I gulped and looked down at the floor as PC Jones left the custody suite, I just stood there not knowing quite what to do or what to expect, a few minutes passed and having looked at and got to know every

A Life on the Lane

speck of dust on the floor I was brought back to reality by the sound of the door opening. The Sergeant burst back into the room his face like thunder. "Stand up straight lad, I am not happy, not happy at all, against my better judgment it would appear that you are going to get a second chance, it seems you either have friends in high places or you are the luckiest person around these parts" the door opened again and in came the PC that had got me from the cell. "Take this urchin out constable and make sure his father is aware of what he has been up to". "OK Sergeant, does that mean he is free to go?" "Yep but I'm not happy about it, I'll lay odds we get him back here before long and when we do I'm going to throw the book at him, I can't understand why the "Super" listened to Constable Jones but that's life, these things happen, just get him out of my sight". "Come on Malcolm let's get you off home with your dad" It was a quiet walk to the car and the journey home was barely any better, my dad didn't really say anything to me, but I knew it was the calm before the storm because I was aware that when we got home he would let rip.

The front door slammed behind us and I ran up the stairs, I don't know why, maybe I thought that if my dad lost his temper it would be less painful if mum was there to put a little control into the situation. Well that was a mistake as I went into the parlour my mum went for me, she caught me an almighty clump around the ear, it was like a hand grenade going off, a loud bang and then the intense pain, but relief came from a totally unexpected source, my dad. He shouted at my mother to stop, maybe I misunderstood his motive I don't know but shouting at my mum was a first. "Just get to your room I don't want to see you" my mum screamed, that was easy and I didn't need to be told twice, it wasn't a punishment it was what I did routinely anyway, I could lose myself in books or comics and get away from the pain and stress of everyday life.

As I lay on top of my bed I could hear my parents, the comments passing between them were full of pain and at times I even felt they were drifting apart, the difficult times I was creating were taking their toll

CHAPTER 6
A BIG IDEA

After my run in with the police life just kind of drifted on, Jack was still at school but we didn't really do a lot together now, quite clearly his father and the situation had brought him to his senses and I had changed somewhat too. PC Richard seemed to be around every corner, it couldn't have been coincidence and to be perfectly honest I didn't really mind that much, him being around did keep me out of trouble on the whole. We would hang around the streets chatting which in itself were good for me, it seemed that the other scallywags noticed that I spent a lot of time with the police and would give me a wide birth. One day he hit upon something that only months previously would have had me in hysterics "have you thought about what you are going to do when you leave school Malcolm?" " No, not really, it always seems so far off , I suppose that I should be like any other kid and say a train driver shouldn't I?" PC Richard laughed "no I don't think so" he replied "you'd have to be on time and that's not going to happen is it?" we both laughed and walked off down All Saints Road. PC Richard continued "I was wondering if you had considered the army or ….?" I stopped him there "the army? You been drinking, me in the army, you know what I'm like with authority, it's bad enough with a strict teacher let alone a bloody Sergeant Major screaming at me, no I don't think so". "Come on Malc you've changed lately your more like your old self, I think you'd be good in the army and the army would be good for you, I was going to suggest the Police but with you being a bloody short arse that's not an option is it?" "I'm tall enough to knock your hat off" and with that jumped up and clouted his helmet. I ran off laughing and shouted "expect I'll see you tomorrow, bye". PC Richard laughed and picked his helmet up "go on you little bugger before I clip your ear" he quipped, "no chance you couldn't catch me". With that I went off home, it was early but I just fancied a quiet evening reading.

When I got home my dad was just pulling up outside and that train driver thing had got me thinking about the old days, my dad would take me to Royal Oak station to see the trains, it was such a memorable part of my life, there was the smell of the steam trains and the chocolate machines on the platform. "Dad do you remember going to see the trains?", "yeah of course I do Malc, why?" "Oh nothing really just been thinking about the old days". My dad had this habit of reading your mind and on this occasion he came up with a suggestion before I could get in with the exact same suggestion. "What you doing now Malc?" "Nothing really why?" "Jump in before your mother see's us", I didn't need asking a second time, I knew where we were going before dad actually told me.

We drove straight to Royal Oak and parked on the bridge over the tracks, oh no there were no yellow lines in those days and what's more, no traffic wardens to worry about. Dad and I went into the ticket hall and got two platform tickets, sounds daft but I could hardly contain myself, this was the first time in years that I had spent time with my dad doing father and son things. We sat down on one of the benches

A Life on the Lane

waiting for an express train to come roaring through on its way to Paddington but first of all what was needed was a bar of Nestles chocolate out of the chocolate machine. I knew dad had conveniently forgotten about the chocolate part of this little outing so it was down to me to use my powers of auto suggestion on him. Twice I got up off the bench and wandered over to the vending machine and twice dad ignored me, but not one to give in I spoke up, "do you remember getting chocolate out of the machine dad?" "No" he replied but he couldn't hold it in anymore, we both burst out laughing, not just a giggle but real lung busting belly laughter that was it, in that moment we reconnected, we had just become father and son again.

After watching half a dozen loco's steaming through it was time to leave but I wanted to do just one more thing, "ere dad you got a penny?", "what's that for then Malc?", "I want to get one of the strip labels from the machine, please dad just a penny". The strip label machine had a big dial with all the letters of the alphabet, numbers and punctuation marks and a pointer arm, select the letters you want, pull down the big handle on the right and print off an aluminium label with raised letters and all for a penny. "Yeah here you are then but that's it no more money tonight." I went off down the platform and printed of my label then ran back to dad clutching my label as I went.

When we got home my mum was fit to burst, "where have you two been, your dinner was ready ages ago it's all cold now, you're lucky it didn't go in the bin". Dad looked at me and I back at him and to my mum's annoyance all we could do was laugh. My mum was completely baffled, so much so she just shook her head and went on ironing without saying another word. Dad and I ate our cold dinner still laughing and giggling like a pair of primary school children, every now and again my mum would look up from the ironing and just look at us in amazement, "sorry mum it's a man thing" I said but all that comment did was bring on more giggling.

After dinner my dad handed me some new comics to read but these were Commando comics not the usual Beano or Dandy, I was a bit surprised I hadn't really read war comics before but then lots of things were different today. I knew this was the best day I'd had for a long time, I hadn't thought I could be that happy again but here I was reading quietly in my bedroom and even now still laughing to myself and with an inner glow I hadn't felt for a long time.

Oh and what's more in case you are wondering I did get a bar of chocolate and it was the best tasting bar of chocolate I have ever eaten. Night came on and the darkness had spread across Notting Hill and for one boy this meant one thing, reading my comics by the light of a torch under my blankets, "oh I've enjoyed today" I said out loud and again I smiled.

It couldn't have been long before I dropped off to sleep but just like the old days when I woke up next morning the torch was turned off along with the comics being placed neatly on the bedside table and under my pillow the aluminium label I'd got from the station. It was silly really the label read "October - Dad and Malcolm"

In the morning I took the label from under my pillow, it was silly but I looked at the label and put it in my pocket, I thought to myself , I'm going to put this away with my special things in my special place. I still had my special hiding place down St Luke's Mews so as soon as I was dressed and ready

A Life on the Lane

for school I ran off down the mews over the piles of rubbish right to the back wall where the loose brick was, I tugged the brick out and pushed my hand in. There were my special things, my small bottle shaped pen knife, a few odd pennies and the two things that I came here to look at once a week at least. Those two things were a small picture of Lin which I had cut from a larger photo and the ring made from the old bottle top that she had given me when we were in Colville school. I took a look at both and a tear came to my eyes even now a few years after her death. I pushed the ring onto my finger but I, unlike Lin had grown up somewhat and it would only go as far as the finger joint. I looked hard at it and had to take it off before I started crying. I carefully packed my treasures back into the hole and along with them added the aluminium label; I pushed the brick back in place and filled the gap around with a handful dirt. I wiped away the tears on my cuff and rubbed the dirt from my hands on my trousers, I giggled as I thought, even at fourteen I was still a dirt magnet.

I scrambled back over the piles of rubbish and set off down the mews towards Basin Street turned left and headed for the bus stop in Westbourne Park Road, I know I had a good day yesterday I thought and I think it could be the start of a new part of my life. I trotted on towards the bus stop and even I noticed that I had got a bit of a spring in my step.

In school everything seemed easier, I began to understand things that had baffled me only a week ago, maths, English and even physics began to be interesting, what on earth was happening to me?

As I sat in a corner of the playground at lunchtime I began to think about what PC Richard had said and I wondered if I might be able to make a go of it in the army, I don't know if it was those commando comics but the more I went over the stories in the comics the more I believed that I should join up. That day I went off home with a career all planned out, I was going to join up as soon as I left school, and I suddenly wanted to be a career soldier and not an ordinary soldier oh no I was going to be a paratrooper. I finished my school day wondering how you went about joining up; I thought about meeting up with PC Richard I was sure he would know all the details.

I caught the number seven bus outside Wormwood scrubs prison but this evening I didn't go straight to the bus stop instead I walked up to the entrance to the prison, I stood there looking at the gates. Those gates that have become an iconic view of British penal justice and I thought what it would be like to hear the doors close behind you for a long period of incarceration. I knew that I had had a lucky escape because had I not come to my senses over the last few weeks chances are I would have ended up listening to the sound of cell doors closing, but still my thoughts went back to Michael who even now was not in prison where he should be. I still believed that one day I would see him suffer and pay for what pain he had put me and Linda's family through. As I turned away from the prison entrance once again I thought about Lin and in a soft voice whispered to myself that even now I still loved her and missed seeing her smiling face, but I took comfort in the fact that I could still hear her laughter and happy voice in my head during the quiet times alone. The voice of one of my class mates Dennis brought me to my senses, "oye Malc wake up mate the bloody bus is coming, get ya finger out", I laughed and ran back down to the bus stop just in time to barge the first year boys out of the way and rush up stairs to the front seat.

Dennis was already up there with Mark and Chris, "blimey Malc, I didn't think you were coming, you were so deep in thought at the prison there we thought you were planning to break in" we all laughed, Dennis was a right case and always had a quip or comment for most situations.

Dennis pulled out a half smoked cigarette and a box of matches and lit up, "want a drag mate?" "No" I replied "I'm giving up, got to think of my health, I'm going to join the Paras". Dennis laughed "what with your record", he quipped. The clippy heard our conversation as she came for the fares and quick as a flash got on Dennis's case, "Well he'd better give up smoking too and make it pretty quick as well, 'cos if he thinks he can get a child's fare while smoking he's got another thing coming. So what is it smoking or child's fare?" I had to laugh she got him bang to rights. "I've finished it anyway" Dennis responded and put the cigarette out, "right then make mine a fourpenny half please darling". "What's yours then soldier boy same as your stupid mates is it?" "Yes please" I replied, "there you go then and I hope you do get in the army, it's a good life my old man was in and he loved it, good luck with it". She turned and walked back down the bus and Dennis threw her a V sign. "I forgot to tell you I've got eyes in the back of my head you little bugger and anymore V signs and you're going to be walking home young man" she didn't break her stride or look back, I have no idea how she saw Dennis's fingers but it gave us all a bloody good laugh. When we got to Westbourne Park Road it was time to get off , Dennis, Mark and Chris went one way and I walked down Basin Street and up St Luke's Mews, for once I wasn't late but still I went straight home.

When I got in mum told me that she had seen Eric, "he asked after you, he reckons you were a good worker on the stall and he still misses you on a Saturday....... Why don't you pop down and see him, he'd love to see you". "Yeah! I'll go down the Lane when I get five minutes, but it's not that easy mum. I know I've been bad towards him and I know it's not his fault but it's been so long now I don't know him anymore, and to be truthful I don't know how to say sorry", with that I went off to my room to get changed.

"I'm going out for a while mum but I'll be back for tea, see you later" I shouted as I headed for the door. "OK but you make sure your not late back or your tea will be in the dog" she replied, that always made me smile, mainly because we didn't have a dog but also because she's been saying that as long as I can remember, "Yeah what-ever mum".

I ran off down the road, this evening I was looking for someone, I actually wanted to see PC Richard. I had made a decision, I had been thinking about it all day and what the bus conductress had said just reinforced what I needed to do, I was going to be a soldier not just any old soldier though I was going to be a paratrooper. Now don't laugh I know that I had been a tearaway in fact a bloody hooligan at times but I knew exactly where I needed to end up, what I didn't know was how to get there. As I walked around the streets in the area looking for my friend the copper I didn't really notice where I was, I had walked up Westbourne Park Road back along St Luke's Road and down Tavistock Road but no sign of PC Richard but I did bump into Michael quite literally, as I banged into him I firstly started to say sorry but when I saw who it was I nearly choked on my words. He was with a couple of other black men both of whom were well into the

A Life on the Lane

six foot heights as was Michael. He had now started to align himself with both English and American black power movements and was quickly becoming a serious nuisance to the Police and residents of the neighbourhood, but that's another story. He looked down at me and I could see that he had recognised the boy that had dared to walk down his road and furthermore had even barged into him. His glare changed and he actually laughed but it was his words that got to me, " I know you boy, you're the one that's from Eric's house, you should be careful or you may get the same as you little girlfriend, now get back to your own kind before I send you back to your mummy in pieces". That was it I flew at him even though I had no chance of ever hurting a man of his build, but that didn't matter my temper had got the better of me, I punched him with all my strength on the chest but it was no good he just laughed. Then from nowhere I felt a strong hand on my collar pulling me backwards, I assumed it was one of his mates but I was wrong, a familiar voice, strong but quiet ordered me to go away. It was PC Richard he had obviously been close by and had seen what was happening, it was probably just as well he was because I had just lost it but with a very dangerous person. Again Richard shouted at me "Go away Malcolm now I won't tell you again", this time was louder and I knew he meant it, I turned and walked towards All Saints Road, I couldn't help it again my feelings got the better of me and I punched a wall in frustration, I was in tears but it was tears of anger. I started to run and got as far as St Luke's mews before I stopped looked around and could see PC Richard hastily trying to catch me, for a moment I wasn't sure that I wanted him to catch me but something inside made me wait. "Malc what on earth are you doing provoking Michael, you know what he is like and since Linda died he has believed that he is untouchable. I've got to tell you, you were lucky tonight, stay away from him and his cronies". "I didn't go looking for him I just bumped into him, literally. I was looking for you, minding my own business when our paths crossed". "Then why were you trying to fight him Malc?" replied Richard. "It was him he started badmouthing Lin and I just couldn't take it". "Alright Malc but please stay away from Tavistock Road and especially Michael I might not be there to look after you next time, now that's the end of it, so why were you looking for me ?".

In all the excitement I had forgotten "I can't remember so it couldn't have been that important, it'll come to me later I expect" I responded. PC Richard must have read my mind because it was him that brought up the subject of what I was going to do when I left school. "Have you given any thought to joining the army?" he said, "no not really" clearly I was lying, it had been on my mind all day, "but I might be open to persuasion if the pay and conditions are right. I'm guessing that if you join an elite part of the army the pay must be better, what about the parachute regiment Richard". Richard laughed "do you really think you would be up to the training Malc?"

It was one of those things that had been in the back of my mind for years, I had watched the Para's training on Wormwood Scrubs lots of times as a kid, I'd seen them jumping from the big blimp type balloon and from airplanes and I guess that somewhere inside me I quite fancied getting me some of the action. "All right Malc, you give it a bit of thought and I'll make some enquiries about the catering corps for you". "You cheeky bugger" I quipped. "Go on get home and I'll see you tomorrow Malc". With that I jumped up and again clouted PC Richards's helmet and this time it

A Life on the Lane

went flying off his head and into the road, "go on then Richard see if you can catch me now" I laughed and sped off down All Saints Road. Richard couldn't help smiling as he picked up his helmet, he didn't even bother to chase me I was well away he just shook his fist at me jokingly.

The next day was Saturday and unlike my normal Saturday I was up early, I had made up my mind to go and see Eric down the Lane, "this was going to be difficult" I said to myself, only it was just loud enough for mum to hear. "Malc it's been a long time since you saw Eric and yes it will be hard but trust me it won't be Eric that makes it difficult, all the difficulties are in your head and in your hands to rectify, it's probably best you get down to see him early before he goes off to dinner and while Paul is still there." "Yeah I know what you mean mum I've just got to pluck up the courage to get it sorted and by the way can I have a couple of bob to get pie and mash for dinner?" "Tell you what Malc you go up to the bakers and get me a loaf of bread while it's still hot and I'll give you a couple of bob for dinner as long as you go and see Eric, deal Malc?" "Yeah, as long as I can have the crust off the hot loaf, deal?" "Yes but don't go nibbling it on the way back", we both had a laugh and mum gave me the money for the bread and off I went still smiling.

I went off up to the bakers shop in Goldbourne Road for the bread, it was a long walk but they baked it on the premises and at this time of the morning it was still hot so with a good fast walk back that crust would still be warm enough to melt the butter when I got back. As I wandered up the lane I spotted a couple of the lads that I used to hang around with, they were hanging around by one of the cafes where you could buy certain mind altering substances, "oye Malc you still hanging out with that copper?" they laughed and I managed to ignore them, I wasn't going to get in an argument today I had better things to do, so I scurried off to howls of derision but I didn't succumb to my urge to shout back, I knew it would end up with me getting a kicking.

When I got the bread I decided to take a different journey home, I would go down the Southam Street area and the halfpenny steps over the railway, that was a grim area, back then the tenements were so overcrowded they made some of "Peter the Poles" places look like the Ritz. It's a funny thing but although the people that lived there were the poorest in the borough I always felt safe and comfortable on the streets and anyway I knew I wouldn't see any of my old mates around those parts. Sure enough I got the loaf home while it was still warm and I got the crust with a thick coating of butter to wander off down the road eating, it seemed as close to perfection as I could get, that bread was so good I can still taste it.

It was about eleven o'clock by the time I got to Eric's stall, which is time for refreshments as I remember, Eric was serving a women so didn't see me approaching the stall, "get your tea for ya mate" I called out to Eric, "yeah why not son" Eric answered without looking up, "Paul, give this young man some tea money will you". Paul looked over and saw who it was, "no governor I'm not sure we can trust this one". Paul winked at me and Eric turned round and looked straight into my eyes and a smile came to his face, "Malc it's good to see you" he walked around the front of the stall and put his arms around me, all he said was "it's been a long time". "Well" I asked "do you want a cuppa Rosie or not?" Paul gave me a handful of change and the tea jug. I set off down the lane

A Life on the Lane

towards Glad's café and couldn't resist making a few extra coppers on the way, "get your tea for ya Stan?" I shouted when I got to the fish stall, "blimey Malc it's been a while ain't it, did you get lost on your way to the café last time?" he joked. "Yeah get us a jug of tea and this time don't take so bloody long coming back". I managed to collect a couple more tea jugs on the way so it was going to be a worthwhile journey; I obviously hadn't lost my touch over the last few years.

When I got to the café Glad's daughter Nora was behind the counter, "hello Malc long time no see, what you been up to?" Nora was in my class at Colville but with all that had been going on I hadn't seen her since we left the old school, "oh nothing much, just hanging around you know what it's like around here?" "Yes I do" she said "but nearly four years of hanging around has to be a new world record, there's a lot of your old mates that would quite like to see you around again Malc", "yeah I'll see what I can do but in the meantime can I have four jugs of tea please?" Nora grinned and started to fill the jugs. Glad was at the till even she recognised me, "hello Malc, good to see you back son, now I'm guessing you want to pay for the jugs one at a time do you, and will you want loads of small change so the stallholders' give you the odd change Malc?". "Yep some things never change Mrs. Peters". She smiled and started to sort out the four piles of money I had placed on the counter. "Bye! Mrs. P and you Nora, see you around". "Of course Malc you know where to find me just don't leave it so long this time". As I left I heard Glad say to Nora "that lads got an eye for you young lady" that made me smile because to be honest I hadn't really thought about girls that much, I suppose they just never measured up to Linda, but I knew that I was starting to move on and after all Nora was a good looking girl.

I walked back down the lane to give the stallholders' their tea and just seemed to be slipping straight back into the market routine. "There you go Mr. Patel one lovely jug of cha", "thank you Malcolm keep the change" he always used to let me keep the change and I of course always made some comment about him only drinking Indian tea. "Thanks Mr. Patel you know don't you that poor Glad had to go all the way to Darjeeling for those leaves I hope you appreciate that", Mr. Patel gave out a raucous laugh "see you haven't changed Malcolm, now piss off you cheeky little bugger". I laughed the swearing sounded so funny with an Asian accent, I laughed again and went on my way but I did wonder if he was actually Indian, you know what he may have been from Pakistan or Timbuktu for all I knew. I got down to Stan's stall and handed over his jug of tea and he of course took the change and turned to serve a punter, "you're still as tight as a duck's arse then Stan" he just laughed and carried on serving as I went down to Eric's. I knew Stan and I knew that he would give me a couple of bob in the afternoon, it was his way of making sure I went back to get his mid afternoon brew. "There you go Eric a nice jug of Rosie for you, anything else I can do?" "Well Malc do you think you remember how to trim the cauliflowers?", "yeah think so". As I got to work I smiled to myself as I realised that I had done it, I had spoken to Eric and what's more I was actually helping out on the stall, I stole a glance at Eric and he too was grinning, seems we both felt we had achieved something today.

As the morning passed into afternoon I trimmed "caulis", polished apples and restocked the stall, I completely forgot about lunch, I still had the money in my pocket that mum

A Life on the Lane

gave me but I was so content I never gave it a second thought. "It's one o'clock Malc, you not having a lunch break today?" questioned Eric as he looked at his pocket watch. Eric never used a wrist watch it was always his pocket watch kept on a shiny gold watch chain, it really did suit him and it was a real pleasure to see it. "Oh yes I just forgot about it". "Where you going?" asked Eric, "mum gave me money for pie and mash, I haven't had it for ages and a few hours ago could hardly wait for lunch, is it OK to shoot off now?". "Well Malc I was wondering if you wouldn't mind me joining you?" "Yeah that would be great Eric"

"Hold the fort Paul, Malc and I are going for a bite back in thirty". Eric took off his money pouch and handed it to Paul, "I want that full up when I get back" he insisted and with that we walked off to the pie and mash shop. "Double pie and mash for the tiddler and I'll have the same but with eels". Eric was in with the order before I could tell him what I wanted but as usual Eric knew best and you know what he was spot on. "This one's on me Malc", "no Eric I've got the money". "Seems you have forgotten that what I say on a Saturday goes, no arguing, this one is on me", it was pointless saying anything else Eric had paid and that was that. We sat on one of the long wooden benches with our plates, I have no idea why but every single pie and mash shop is the same, long bench seats holding about six people and long marble tables. Maybe it's a London thing but there was no embarrassment or apprehension about sitting at a table with up to ten complete strangers to eat your dinner and what's more by the time you had finished you knew them by name, now that's community for you.

Eric and I got stuck into our grub, this was one of those

halcyon days I have heard people wax lyrical about and between scoops of food I managed to let Eric know how I felt about this feast I was enjoying.

"Can I ask you a question Eric?" "Well only if you're not asking for a sub, you get paid in arrears in the market trade Malc". I giggled a bit which were probably juvenile nerves, "No it's not that, it's just that as I remember Saturday lunchtime was horse racing, I just wondered if you still dabbled". Eric looked at me and rather unexpectedly he smiled. "I just wondered Eric, it worries me after what happened before," "don't worry Malc I haven't had a bet since Linda died, I knew that my actions that day and my stupid attempt to make a quick buck was as much to blame as anything else and I have to live with it every day, now what about you, I keep my ears to the ground Malc and I know what you've been up to and I was surprised with some of what has gone on, but I know you're a good boy inside and now it's time for that good boy to grow up into a good man." "Yeah I know Eric; I've not been the best I could've been". "Let me stop you there Malc, you know that you've been misguided which is good, it means you understand the difference between right and wrong, so that's half the battle won. What do you think Lin would think of what you became, she would have nothing to do with someone that was in trouble with the police and running the streets out of control...?" " Hang on Eric I did some naughty stuff but I never hurt no one, some of it was just high jinks a bit of a laugh". "What you saying Malc that you look up to people like Michael because they hurt people, does that make them better than the little people around here. If I were a betting man I'd say that Michael started off just like you but you've got more brain power than him and you've seen where this

A Life on the Lane

behaviour is leading you. I'm proud of that Malc and I'm proud of you, I know you are going to do the right thing." I did start to think that this was turning into a lecture but deep down inside I knew Eric was right, it's funny but I realised that one of the reasons I wanted to talk to Eric again was to get his approval and what he had said gave me that reassurance, I also wanted to talk to him about the army, again I think I needed his backing in just the same way I wanted my dad's.

"Eric I wanted to run something by you, it's a bit silly really but I know you won't laugh at me, well not too much anyway". I started fiddling with the vinegar bottle, turning it round so the bottom scraped on the marble table, Eric reached across and put his huge calloused hand over mine and the bottle. "Malc what-ever you need to say I won't laugh but if you keep spinning that bottle around and break it old Len Houghton will be out of that kitchen quicker than you can say Sarsons and you will get a flat hand around your ear sure as eggs is eggs". I laughed and set the bottle down in the middle of the table, "right Eric well it's like this", Eric looked at me intently and I continued, "I've been talking to PC Richard and he reckons I could do a lot worse than joining the army, well I'm not sure he's far from the truth, he thinks it could be the making of me, you know make a man of me like you said I needed to think about". "Well Malc that's going to take some getting used to, look the times getting on let's talk about it on the way back to the stall". Eric and I slid ourselves out from the bench, as we walked towards the door I caught the eye of Beryl the Saturday girl in the pie and mash shop. "Hello Malc you alright?" she asked, "yeah I'm OK Beryl, you?" "Yes! Good" she responded, Eric looked at me and shook his head "you like the girls don't you Mac?" "Well Eric if you've got it and all that".

Eric pushed me towards the door and once outside I pursued the army subject again. "Yeah Eric I was thinking about the Parachute regiment". Eric took a sharp intake of breath and stopped in his tracks, "Malc don't do that, for a minute there I thought you said the Parachute regiment". "I did and you said you wouldn't laugh". "Well Malc there's an awful lot of training to be done if you want to make it in the Paras..." I stopped Eric there, "the last person that questioned whether I was up to the training had his pointy hat knocked in to the road", we both laughed and Eric pointed out that he was taller than PC Richard and that he didn't wear a pointy hat. We carried on walking and laughing, Eric reassured me that he believed in me and that the army was a good idea, "yeah I'm sure you would do well in the army, you should talk to your dad about it Malc, he was an army man you know, what was his regiment, he told me once, based at the Tower as I remember". "That's right he was in the Fusiliers". "Don't you fancy the Fusiliers then Malc?" "I just feel I want to do something special, you've seen them practicing over the "Scrubs", you must know what I mean?" "Yeah! Of course I do, you're right you must follow your dreams and anyway I know you Malc if you set your mind to it you will make a go of it. Now what about doing a bit of selling on the stall for an hour or so?" I was taken aback, Eric had never let me sell from the stall before, I was only ever there in a behind the scenes capacity. "Yeah! Yeah of course Eric, are you sure?" "Well Malc we were just talking about your journey into manhood so let's just say this is the first step on that journey, after all if you are going to join the Paras and save the world, selling a few spuds from the stall is going to be child's play". "Yeah! You got it Eric, child's play, that's why you're so good at it". I ran off laughing "see you back at the stall Eric".

A Life on the Lane

When I got back to the stall Paul had a queue of women waiting to be served, "it's a good job I rushed back Paul, Eric said I should start serving customers seems you're a bit slow these days", "you cheeky "little git", I'll give you slow" Paul smiled, "go on then get serving if you think you're as good as me and if you think you can reach the bags". The bags were on a steel hook hanging from the top beam of the stall so they were about six feet up and a little forward of where you stand to serve, in the old days they were way out of reach but I had grown a bit over the last few years so I reached up and snatched a bag from the hook. "Looks like you're tall enough after all Malc. Now let's see how the ladies get on with you."

I hadn't seen Eric come back to the stall; he was still grinning and pushed me forward towards the next customer. "Yes love what can I get for you?" I said in a strong and confident voice - that was it half the market burst out laughing, including me. "I'll have a pound of apples please." The first customer was going to be easy I thought, "What you after then Grannies or lovely red Cox's?" I was growing in confidence with every breath "Oh I like a nice red "Cox" young man" the women said. I of course didn't get the innuendo anywhere near quick enough and again everyone around burst into laughter, that's twice I thought to myself but I did not expect the third one to come along straight after. Being careful what I said I responded "OK! The red ones it is then." I stretched across to the pile of Cox's apples and popped four of them on one side of the scales and the brass one pound weight on the other. "Look at that" I said "spot on". I opened the brown paper bag and slid the four apples in and with a flick of the wrist spun the bag to seal it – wrong - in front of everyone as I spun the bag the bottom split and the bloody apples flew across the stall and rolled across the pavement. It was mayhem everyone was in absolute stitches including me I have to add.

CHAPTER 7
AN APPOINTMENT TO KEEP

Monday morning came around and mum got me up for school as usual, these days I didn't need much persuading the fact that I had started understanding the lessons meant that I actually started to enjoy them. As soon as mum called, I was out of bed and in the bathroom, but like most boys my age I wasn't brilliant at the personal hygiene stuff. Oh I did it, but a one minute brush of the teeth seemed like an eternity so I may be managed thirty seconds. I got myself very wet however mainly because that way I assumed that mum would think I had got myself nice and clean for the day ahead, getting myself that wet of course meant that the towel got equally wet another sign that I had done a thorough job at my ablutions, then it was dress and grab a slice of toast and away to the bus stop.

I always got the earlier bus now instead of having to rush to get to school on time but this morning I bumped into PC Richard. "Hi Malc you OK?" "Yeah! I'm good glad I've seen you" I replied. "Why's that Malc need to get your fix of knocking my helmet off do you?" PC Richard laughed, "I haven't given you a clip round the ear for the last time yet you little bugger." "No! Nothing like that, I wanted to have a chat about the army, but I guess you will be off shift when I get off school." "That's not a problem Malc drop into the market café after school and we can chat then, see you at about four thirty?" "Yeah! That'll be great thanks mate, sorry officer." "Go on get off to school Malc, your bus is coming, run or you'll miss it". Sure enough when I looked up the number seven bus was on its way down Westbourne Park Road and I was a hundred yards or more from the stop and there was no one else waiting, so chances are it wouldn't stop unless I made it to the stop first, there was only one thing for it and it's a good job I'm young and fit I thought. The day at school went well I managed to understand all that I was supposed to and didn't get into any trouble which meant no detention; it would have been sods law to get detention on the day I was meeting up with Richard.

It was about four o'clock when the bus home arrived and all the boys from school got on, there was never a queue it was more like a rugby scrum but on most occasions me and my mates would be amongst the first on so as to get up the front seats on the upper deck and today was no exception. The bus trundled off along Du Cane Road and up came the conductor, he was a big West Indian chap, twopenny half was the repeated request from all the boys on the bus and each one got the same question "where you getting off man?" and each one gave the same reply "Barlby Road". I of course along with Chris, Mark and Dennis would go to Westbourne Park Road but and here is the catch, we had all to a man spent the extra two pence needed for the correct fare. "Twopenny half please" I requested. "Where you going to man, no don't tell me Barlby Road?" "Yeah! Spot on mate Barlby Road", then we settled back for a chat till we got to our stops. The bus arrived at Barlby Road and to all our surprise the conductor called out Barlby Road, nothing we all

A Life on the Lane

stayed exactly where we were. "Barlby Road" came the call again, then we heard the footsteps coming up the stairs and at the top the conductor again called "Barlby Road and this bus is going nowhere until all you twopenny halves get off". Most of the kids stood up and got quietly off, but the four of us at the front stayed and just continued looking out of the front window and ignoring the conductor. "I said all the twopenny halves have had their money's worth and it is time to get off the bus, now!" Chris, Dennis, Mark and I looked at the conductor and he was not smiling, "alright mate we're going" Dennis responded, and we got up to leave the bus. Oh shit I thought I'm going to be late meeting Richard now, so once off the bus's platform I pulled my duffle bag into my shoulder and started running, "see you lads - I've got an appointment, "gotta run" - and I set off down St Marks Road.

The jog home was going fine until I reached Lancaster Road and I ran into a bunch of lads from Isaac Newton school, back then there was a lot of rivalry between schools and sometimes this ended in shall we say "fisticuffs" - "oh bollocks" - I said out loud, I knew what the outcome of this coming together would be and as I was on my own I got the distinct impression it was going to be me that would come off worse. "I don't suppose it's worth saying sorry, is it, because I'm thinking you Isaac Newton "thicko's" have no idea what that means anyway, do you?" That was not the most intelligent thing to say was it, I thought but it was done now and in the split second before they realised what I had said I started to run. Now I'm not slow but one of the kids was on me in seconds, I felt a punch to the back of the head and I stumbled and ended up in a heap in the gutter and the others kids were on me like a pack of dogs. I felt the kicks come in and I curled up in a ball, I can look after myself but from the

83

position I was in fighting back probably wasn't an option, I just had to take the kicks and hope they got bored with this game sooner rather than later. After a few more kicks I heard someone shout at the kids "oye get off him you animals" the boys looked around to see an old man coming towards them, he must have been about eighty but I don't know if it was surprise or the fact that in those days people still held a certain amount of respect for their elders but they had it on their toes and ran off down the road. The old man gave me a hand up and looked at my face "you're going to have a "nice shiner" there son and a fat lip; you better get home and get yourself cleaned up."   I looked at the old man "thanks mate, it's a good job you came along I was about to really do them some damage" I said, "yeah! I could see that" he replied and with that hobbled off.

I got to the café about fifteen minutes late and in a right state but fortunately PC Richard had waited, "bloody hell Malc what you been up to?" Richard enquired.   "I had to teach a gang of Isaac Newton kids to be polite." "Did they listen Malc?" "To be quite honest PC Richard I didn't actually get to start the lesson".   Richard laughed, "Well you are going to have a lovely black eye tomorrow, you got a steak to put on Malc's eye Glad?" "No! We don't do meals at this time of night, but he can have a bottle of coke that'll do the trick."   I whispered to Richard "I'm skint, I can't pay for it," "it's on me Malc, don't worry, now what were we going to talk about Malc?"   "It's about the army. I've been giving it a bit of thought and I'm really up for it but before you laugh at me like everyone else I want to join the Paras." "I'm not going to laugh Malc, I've seen what you are capable of and I know if you set your mind to it you can do anything."   The conversation continued for a good half hour, me telling

A Life on the Lane

Richard how I was going to be the best Para the world could imagine and Richard listening to everything intently, not once did he laugh, he actually seemed like he believed me. "OK! Malc calm down now, don't get too excited you are going to have to wait a year or two and the way your brain flips from one thing to another the chances are you're going to have other ideas before you are old enough to sign up." "Oh no Richard this is it for me, like you said when I set my mind to something it is always going to happen." "Alright then Malc let me find out a bit more then maybe I'll pop round and see your mum and dad, now get off home and don't blame me if your suppers cold." "Thanks Richard, I knew you'd listen" and with that I left the café and ran full of "the joys of spring" to get my supper and a smile a mile wide across my face.

Things had started going really well lately, most Saturdays I went down the lane and did a few hours on Eric's stall, and I even managed to catch a game of football now and again, I'd always been a QPR fan but for one reason or another didn't go to the games that often. It was still a time when Rangers had a great team so the crowds were big, a game of football is always best when you are squashed together on a cold packed terrace, I can't be doing with sitting in the stands it's just not the same, all of which made me think about some of my old mates, Freddy, Bobby and all the Clydesdale house football team. It was only a joke, we weren't really a football team just the boys that had a kick about on a Sunday morning in the football enclosure behind the flats. I wonder if they still play a bit, that's it come Sunday I'm going to pop over the flats for a kick about, I thought.

Sunday morning came around and I was up with the larks, I had breakfast, got cleaned and dressed and found a pair of pumps to wear, "where you off to in them Malc?" mum asked. "Thought I'd pop over the flats see if the lads are having a kick about." "Oh that's a good idea Malc, Freddy asked if you still played apparently some of the boys are playing in a team now on a Sunday morning, I'm sure if you hurry over the flats Freddy will still be there." "Yeah! I will, thanks mum gotta run," and with that I was sprinting down the stairs and out of the front door. I ran across the road and into the flats, I got to Fred's front door and gave it an almighty thump. Mrs. Fish came to the door curlers in her hair and a fag hanging out of the corner of her mouth. "Blimey Malc long time no see." " Yeah! It's been a while but I'm back now, anyway is your little brother Freddy in?" "Little brother, ha! ha! you still got the blarney then you little bugger, yeah he's here come in he's just getting his football stuff together." I followed her into the hall and in her usual soft and gentle bellowing screech she yelled up the stairs, "Fred, you got a visitor are you ready yet?" "Yeah! Just coming tell Kit to hang on a second." After a few minutes Freddy sauntered down the stairs, "you're early Kit; it's not like you to be ready first." "Hi Freddy how's tricks" I quipped, Freddy stopped dead on the bottom stair, "Christ Malc what have I done to deserve this then?" he said. "Yeah! Sorry it's been a while but I've had a lot on my plate lately but hey I'm back now."

I got the impression that he wasn't actually that pleased to see me but then I suppose that's not really surprising, I hadn't been the best of mates for a while. "I just wondered if you guys still have a kick about in the enclosure on Sunday mornings." "Not during the season, me, Kit and some of the others joined a proper team so we play Sunday mornings," there was a bit of a pause and a little reluctantly and with the

A Life on the Lane

help of a sideways glance from his mum Freddy asked if I wanted to come along, "look you ain't gonna get a game but you could meet the others and the manager might want to try you out for the team, think you can keep up with us?" It was his turn to be sarcastic now, Mrs. Fish laughed and this time it was a real laugh that turned into a tar filled nicotine flavoured cough, "ere Mrs. F if I was twenty years older I'd offer to rub some winter green on that chest of yours." Freddy looked at me "oye you can't say that to my mum it ain't right." Mrs. Fish laughed even more which made the coughing worse to the point that the cigarette end on her lips flew across the hallway, Freddy picked it up off the lino and handed it back to his mum, "see you later mum, I'll be back for dinner, bye" and with that we were off to Kit's flat. Kit lived two doors up from Fred so it was just a second before I had to go through the same, "where have you been" stuff and of course the answers and the apologies remained the same, but actually this time Kit seemed genuinely pleased to see me, I guess he would be though because maybe I had been more of a bastard to Freddy than I had to Kit.

The three of us set off to walk to Paddington Recreation Ground which I can tell you is a fair old trot but before we got two hundred yards up the road it was like we hadn't been living separate lives, we laughed, joked, kicked a tin can down the road and generally acted like a group of mates. The joviality was broken by Freddy shouting out at the top of his voice "Oh bollocks, with all the distractions we've gone and forgotten Bobby". All three of us burst out laughing "how the bloody hell can we forget the goalkeeper" giggled Freddy, "well don't look at me I'm the shortest of all of us and I've only got pumps on and no kit". "Don't worry Malc we wouldn't expect you to go in goal and anyway you ain't signed up". Bobby must have heard us laughing because within a few minutes he had caught us up. "You bastards I thought you were going to call for me, oh hi Malc you alright, I didn't know you were coming to play".   Bobby didn't change his tone and didn't seem to have noticed that I hadn't been around for some time.   "Ahh... yeah sorry about that mate but I was so gob smacked to see the prodigal son here that I just screwed up on the arrangements" Freddy admitted. "Oh never mind lads I was a bit late getting ready anyway, so you in the team today or not Malc" Fred looked at Bobby "you're bloody hard work Bob, I just told you he ain't signed up so he can't play and anyway he might not want to". "Yeah I do Fred....but let's see what your manager has to say about it shall we".

The four of us carried on laughing and joking, kicking anything on the pavement that wasn't either too hard or too soft which ruled out bricks and dog shit but .... Have you ever noticed how small dogs can do the business and the hard round bits look just like pebbles but when kicked the hard crust breaks and the softer inner spreads around the toe of your lovely pumps, yes I found out the hard way. Fred and Kit had a bloody good laugh at that but Bobby in his usual manor just looked at the mess on my shoe and said straight faced "I done that" "oh you dirty git" the three of us answered in unison "no no not the shit I mean.... oh yeah I get it your just taking the Mick, ha bloody ha". I found a bit of old newspaper and wiped off what I could and we got on our way again.

When we got to the rec Freddy introduced me to the manager "ere boss this is Malc, he used to be a bit useful up front and he wanted to know if we are looking for new players" "you know this lot Freddy there's always someone

A Life on the Lane

that forgets it's Sunday morning, so if he's reliable, yeah bring him along to training Wednesday and we can see just how useful he is." Freddy, Kit and I wandered off towards the changing rooms and once again we had forgotten Bobby, "Freddy what's happened to Bobby" I asked "He's over by the pitch chatting up the birds, he won't get changed until the boss shouts at him" I looked over and could see Bobby hands going ten to the dozen and laughing out loud but as he moved around the girls I was taken aback to see that the dark haired girl that had been facing the pitch with her back to me had looked around and was staring at me, I was taken aback because I had recognised her, this was another bit of my past that I was avoiding. Although the years had passed and at times had dragged beyond belief I never went more than a few minutes without thinking about Lin and there not twenty five yards away was the biggest reminder of Lin there could be. Sue was looking straight at me, she looked deep into my eyes, I could feel her looking at my very soul, and I did not know what to do. Sue was Linda's best friend, they had been almost as inseparable as we had been and to bump into her meant that all the hurt was bubbling back to the surface, I felt tears welling up in my eyes, god no I thought, I haven't prepared myself for this but there she was. I turned around and walked towards the gate but I didn't get far before I felt a hand on my shoulder, it was Bobby, " Oye Malc where you going it's kick off in ten minutes you getting changed" "No Bobby your manager ain't got a place for me today so I'm going to get off home". Bobby looked at me and for once I could tell he had read between the lines and was letting his real self out. "There's no need to run away Malc I ain't as green as most people think, we all know how much you've been hurting and Sue feels the same but you gotta move on now, don't hurt Sue more by ignoring her, go and at least say hello" "I wasn't running away Bobby I didn't recognise her, I thought it was just some bird you were chatting up" I gulped deeply and assured Bobby now I knew who it was I was going to nip over and say hi. "Good it'll help the pair of you but you keep your bloody hands off her mate because I think I might be in there, anyway I'd better get my kit on or the boss will be using one of my balls in his whistle instead of a pea." I laughed and turned back towards the pitch as Bobby ran off to the changing room.

It was only twenty five yards or so to where Sue was standing but every step allowed me time to fear the meeting, what was I going to say, did Sue blame me and could I stop myself from shedding a few tears. It wasn't long before I found out and it wasn't an anti climax, "hi Sue, sorry I didn't recognise you" "that's alright Malc I wasn't sure it was you either, so how you been then?" "well it's been a bit of a journey but I'm getting there, what about you" "Well Malc to be honest I wish that I had been selfish enough to run away from everything and everyone but I wasn't, I hung around shed a million tears and tried to come to terms with losing my best friend." I knew what she meant and of course she was right but before I had time to feel too sorry for myself Sue apologised, "I'm sorry Malc I know what you've been through and from what I hear you are making a go of it again, I just didn't know what I was going to say when I saw you standing there, it is good to see you again Malc, honest". That was worse than her anger, I felt the tears coming and I struggled to stop myself bawling, "look Sue I'm not running away but I'm going home now, I was only popping out to see Freddy and ended up here, I'll see you soon though Sue... I promise", and with that I turned and walked away. I had only gone a few steps when I turned to look at Sue, she in turn was doing

A Life on the Lane

the same thing, she smiled and waved I could see the glint of a tear and the sparkle of happiness in her eyes. "Oh and say hello to your mum for me" I blurted out "and I forgot to say Bobby's got eyes for your mate there" the girl with Sue blushed and giggled "yeah and she holds a candle for him too" Sue responded "shut up, no I don't" the other girl insisted, with that I turned and sprinted away.

Monday morning came and it was back to school which of course I didn't mind because school had now become my sanctuary, not many people knew about my private life and to be honest I don't actually think they cared much. I went through the day thinking about Sue and recognised the feelings I was getting, of late I hadn't been shy of chatting up girls and in fact was quite good but Sue had made me feel all wobbly, I know that's not a scientific term for how I felt but it just seemed to sum it up. Every time I thought about her I went wobbly, I think that's pretty succinct. I decided to go over and see her as soon as possible which of course meant after school but what excuse could I use, just popped over to see your mum? Do you have any pictures of Linda? Oh I don't know but I thought I'll just hoof it, us market boys are good at the patter so something would turn up.

That evening after school I went to Sue's, I walked over the road and got to the bottom of the outside stairs but as of that moment I had no idea what I was going to say, but it was like someone was looking over me because as I raised my left leg to the first step the front door opened and Sue and the girl from the park appeared in the door way. Sue looked down at me and her eyes lit up. Quick as a flash I thought of something to say "oh glad your mates here I've got a message from Bobby for her" - now her eyes lit up. "Oh yeah what's that then?" "Well" I said "if I'm passing on messages I need to know I'm telling the right person, so what's your name?" They responded in unison "Rita" "that's good then" I replied; "Bobby said tell Rita he's going down to St Marks park Wednesday for football practice and he wanted to meet you down there after". The pair of them giggled and I turned to leave I still didn't really know how to carry on the conversation with Sue but it was like she was psychic or something, before I could go more than a step she asked whether I was going to football as well, I knew exactly why she asked and I responded positively. "Yeah I'm going to try out for the team, I'm going to try and get fit again," Rita retorted "I know someone that thinks your fit enough already." Sue went as red as a beetroot and giggled; I laughed and made a hasty retreat. Now the only problem was breaking the news to Bobby that he had a date after football on Wednesday, I chuckled and under my breath said to myself "no tell him once we get down the park Wednesday." I ran off home for my tea and knew that evening I would stay in and do my homework, and then as I've always done, go to my room and read.

When I got home mum was in the kitchen preparing tea, so I called out a quick hello as I went to my room to change out of my uniform, "Malc you're not going out are you" mum responded. "No why?" "PC Richard came round today and he wants to see you, he said he would drop by at about six." I knew what he was coming for because you could rely on Richard, I felt sure that he would be bringing information on the army.

I suppose that being a copper meant that time and timing were important because as the clock on the living room

A Life on the Lane

mantelpiece chimed for six the door bell rang. "I'll get it mum, that must be PC Richard." I ran off down the stairs and answered the door and sure enough PC Richard was standing there. "Hello Malc" he was in before me with the greeting, "hello constable what can I do for you then?" "Well first off you can invite me in; I haven't got a search warrant and secondly get the kettle on." "Of course come on in." I ushered Richard in front of me "go on up, you know the way, mum's in the kitchen she can make a pot of Rosie." "You lazy little bugger Malc you make the tea" Richard responded, "I've come to see you not your mum," "yeah OK I'll make the tea enough of the nagging."

Richard got to the flat and went inside and headed straight for the kitchen where mum was, "Good evening Mrs. Williams how are you, keeping well I hope?" - Blimey I thought - he's being polite, "hello again Richard, yes I'm fine would you like a nice...?" I laughed and Richard turned and looked in my direction, "yes please Mrs. Williams, Malc and I have already chatted about it and he was saying how he enjoys making the tea when people come around, isn't that right Malc?" "Yeah that's right I'll make it mum - white with two sugars Constable?" Richard laughed and was ushered out of the kitchen and into the living room by my mum.

I could hear the two of them chatting but couldn't actually hear what was being said, I finished making the tea and went into the living room and the conversation stopped. Mum looked up and gave me a smile "OK" I said "what you been talking about?" I asked. Mum was first in to answer "Richard was telling me about the army Malc and what is involved, I just didn't realise how close it was to happening for you. I can't help thinking that my little boy is on the verge of becoming a man." "Oh mum that sounds so well mum like." That made us all laugh.

CHAPTER 8
A CAREER IN THE ARMY ?

Richard and I sat in the front room and went over what was involved in becoming a Para and for the first time I started to wonder if I was up to the task, first there was being accepted for such an elite branch of the army, then there was the training. Richard told me about the hill and the bridge and the bloody great tree trunks the recruits had to carry, he told me about the PTI's that would push you to the absolute brink and he told me about the route marches in full kit with a rifle and full back pack. Then of course there was the prospect of being shot at in some God forsaken outpost of the empire by someone that probably didn't even wear a uniform but just enjoyed taking pot shots at yours.

"All in all this army thing may not be such a good idea" I said to Richard, "ah that's the point you see Malc, you get nothing for nothing. They need to make sure that you are serious before spending God knows how much on uniform, equipment, training and then sending you off to some exotic far off part of the world to enjoy yourself. You see you need to realise that if you join up you are joining the army and soldiers sometimes have to go to war and that means putting your life on the line, it's that serious Malc."

"I know Richard and I am serious, it's just that I am wondering if I'm up to it, if there's one thing that frightens me its failure. I've gone and told everyone I'm joining the Paras so now I've got to go through with it and what's more important is I'm going to do it for Linda, she would have hated to see me wasting my life." "Well Malc that's the best reason I've heard so far."

PC Richard stood up "I'll leave you to think about it a bit more and look through the literature and then if you want I'll talk to your dad and he can pop in to see your Careers Officer at school if you want" - "yeah that would be great Richard thanks." Richard left the living room and headed for the kitchen to say goodbye to my mum before leaving, "I've got to go now Mrs. Williams but I've left some literature with Malc maybe you and Mr. Williams can have a look at it and see what you think." "Of course PC Richard, Malc's dad should be home soon so we can talk about it then, thanks for all your doing for Malcolm we all appreciate it" and with that Richard headed off down the stairs towards the front door with me following on behind.

When we got to the front door Richard opened it and was greeted by my dad desperately trying to chase the door inward as the key was wrenched from his hand. "Oh sorry Mr. Williams I didn't hear you there" PC Richard said, "that's alright PC Jones but that is certainly a powerful pull you have there, I thought it was Superman coming out of the house" - they both laughed and Richard went out on to the street, he turned to talk to dad. "Mr. Williams I have left some literature with Malc about the army, I thought it would be good for you to go over it with him, you know he is really keen on this one and with your military experience I thought you could give him the low down on it." "Of course I'll have a

A Life on the Lane

chat with Malc when I've looked it over." my dad replied. "OK, goodnight Mr Williams, Malc see you around and thanks for the tea" and with that he turned and walked off down the road.

As my dad and I walked up the stairs he put his arm around my shoulder and smiled at me, "let's go and have dinner shall we?" he said, "yeah I'm starving, what-ever we've got it smells good, I thought PC Richard was going to ask to stay for some food while we were sitting in the living room chatting". I smiled back at dad as we went into the kitchen.

"Hello love had a busy day?" my mum always called him love unless there was a row in the air then it was John, "yeah too many picky housewives, everyone wants the best meat for the lowest price, I can tell you I wish I had a penny for every time someone told me the last joint they had was all fat and gristle. It's a wonder anyone ever eats any meat." "Oh never mind I made you a lovely stew with that beef you brought home yesterday and do you know what, by the time I had cut off all the fat and gristle there was nearly enough meat left to make three hearty bowl's full." Dad retorted "you cheeky moo, it's a good job I love you" and with that he planted a kiss right on her lips. "Oh yuk" I said "you pair are far too old for that sort of stuff." I went to the bathroom and washed my hands ready to eat.

At the dinner table my dad looked across to me and asked "are you serious about the army Malc because it's a big decision to make, it won't be easy you know." "I know that dad but it's something I want to do, I've given it a lot of thought over the last month or so and I really think it's the right way to go." "Well in that case Malc we should give those brochure a look tonight, it's the Fusiliers you wanted to join wasn't it?" "No dad you know it's the Para's." "Oh, ok Malc but I was kind of hoping you would choose my old regiment son, still it's your choice and I am sure you will make me proud what-ever you choose." "Thanks Dad it will mean a lot to me if you're happy with it." Mum then chirped up "do I get a say in all this?" Dad and I looked at her and could see that she had a tear in her eye. "I just feel that this is all happening without me having a say in what happens to my little boy, oh I know your growing up fast Malc but to me you are still a little boy, my little boy. You have seen things that children shouldn't see and at the end of it you have turned out OK but, but...." Mum got up and left the room, clearly she had become very tearful, I looked down at the bowl of stew in front of me and at that point I realised that a family was more than just the sum of its individual members, we all added our own personalities and traits to the whole which bonded us all together no matter what life threw at us. Dad went into the bedroom where mum had gone; I could hear voices although not what was being said. I picked at my food until mum and dad came back into the kitchen.

"I'm sorry Malc" - mum seemed better now even though her eyes were still red, "it's just me being silly, but these last few years have just gone by so quickly, every time I look at you, well you have grown a little more and now I am looking at a young man not a little boy anymore and what a fine young man you have become." I got up and hugged her she whispered in my ear "what a fine young man you have become."

After reading the bits and pieces that PC Richard had left I decided to go ahead and see the careers adviser at school even though I knew it was too soon, so on Monday lunchtime

A Life on the Lane

I sniffed out Mr. Toms - Mr. Toms was a mountain of a man who looked after the careers department at school. "Ere Mr. Toms can I have a chat about careers" Mr. Toms who was about 3 feet taller than me always had a sarcastic quip, he looked around pretending not to see me "I must be losing it" he whispered "I thought I heard a voice but there's no one here" and he turned to walk away. "OK Mr. Toms very funny, it's me Malcolm Williams." Mr. Toms looked round and down. "Oh thank the Lord for that Mr. Williams I thought I was hearing things but then that happens quite a lot when you little people are around."

I laughed more to amuse Mr. Toms than because it was funny, if I had heard it once I had heard it a thousand times; he used the same lines over and over again with the boys. "Anyway Mr. Williams what can I do for you?" "Well I have really started to think about what I am going to do when I leave school and had really set my sights on the army, the parachute regiment." "Mr. Williams what can I say I am glad to hear that you are thinking and thinking about a career at that, so do you want to make an appointment to talk over joining my old regiment?" I looked up at Mr. Toms "your Regiment...? I had no idea but yes, yes I want to come and talk it over with my dad." Mr. Toms reached into his breast pocket and pulled out a small pocket diary "and when would you like to have this cosy little chat then?" "Well" I said "it's got to be a Thursday afternoon because my dad works in a shop and Thursday is half day closing." "OK Mr. Williams Jr. what about this Thursday at the end of lessons?" "Yeah! That sounds good Thursday it is then.... Oh can I confirm that tomorrow because I just need to make sure Mr. Williams Senior is available?" With that I sped off to join the lads playing with a tennis ball in the playground.

Now this will amuse anyone that went to Christopher Wren School because that tennis ball had a profound effect on us kids, you see dividing the playgrounds were single bars set about a foot off the ground which seemed to have no sensible use with one exception. The Bar Game, now the bar game is a game of skill something like tennis except that the idea was to hit the bar and hopefully get the rebound for a second or subsequent throw at the bar, scoring was exactly the same as tennis. This has left me with one pretty worthless skill, the ability to throw a tennis ball at a metal bar with a decent bit of accuracy. I am sure that some time in the future it's a skill that will come in handy, well maybe not!

The afternoon's lessons passed without incident and I was anxious to get off home to tell mum that I had made an appointment to see Mr. Toms; I knew that I would still have to wait for dad to come in from work just to make sure he wasn't busy Thursday afternoon. Thursday afternoons meant one thing to my dad and that was the cinema, he loved going off to see a film by himself, back then there wasn't anywhere near as many films on the TV in fact the only time they showed films was Sunday afternoon and Christmas, but even so we loved the old cowboy or war films that were shown in black and white on a tiny TV set.

That afternoon I went straight home, I was buzzing I simply couldn't wait for dad to come home to see if he could make it to school to see Mr. Toms. When I got in mum was doing some housework as usual, don't ask me what, all I know is, it involved her singing at the top of her voice and shuffling around in the kitchen. Mum heard the door and called out to me, "that you Malc – you're early no detention?" "Oh very funny" I responded "you know I'm a reformed character, I

A Life on the Lane

haven't had detention in ages," "I know Malc I was only joking." Mum started singing again and it was my excuse to make a quick exit, I went to my bedroom to change and as soon as I had it was comic time, I just decided that was preferable to getting under my mum's feet. After an hour or so things started to smell good in the kitchen department so I knew that it wouldn't be long before dad got home. "Malc you going to get washed ready for dinner your dad will be home any minute so I'll be dishing up soon," I didn't need telling twice the comic was slung under the bed and I rushed into the bathroom, I must have thought that washing your hands made time fly.

It wasn't long after washing that I heard the front door open and without another word I was down the stairs, without touching a step on the top flight I got to the front door before my dad could get inside, "dad you're not going to the flicks Thursday afternoon are you?" "Crikey son let me get in the door" - "OK dad but it's really important." I turned and started off up the stairs until I heard the door close - "well dad you're not going to the pictures Thursday are you?" - "well yes I am actually there's a new John Wayne film on at the Odeon so I was going to catch that, why do you want to know?" "Oh well I have made an appointment to see our careers master at school and it's for this Thursday afternoon." Dad looked at me and took a sharp intake of breath, "well Malc it is John Wayne and you know how much I like going to see a film ......" dad paused "but well for something as important as that I can miss just one film," "thanks dad" and with that I ran back up the stairs. "Malc you need to ask your mum to come to the meeting too, this is just as important to her you know" – "yeah of course dad ... I was going to, I just wanted to make sure you could make it." Now I just had to wait until Thursday two days was going to seem an awfully long couple of days.

The next day at school came and went but the evening was going to be special, again I started to feel wobbly as I went over to Freddy's flat. This time I wasn't the first there, Kit was already hanging around outside waiting for Freddy. "Alright Kit" which was our usual greeting, "yeah cushty mate, Freddy's just coming" and with that the door opened and Freddy appeared. "Malc, Kit everything OK" "yeah lets go" I replied. "No, no, I... we forgot Bobby again." "Don't worry" Kit said "he'll catch us up he always does" - "well" I said "he's going to have a shock when he does, because I made a date for him with that girl Sue was with on Sunday... and he doesn't know yet." That tickled Kit and Freddyy and we set off laughing as we walked off towards the park.

We had only got as far as Portobello Road when Bobby came running down the road after us. "Oye you lot ain't you ever going to wait for me?" Freddy turned round and responded "and ain't you ever going to be on time especially when you got a date to keep?" "It's not that important, it's only practice," the three of us laughed and Kit just added a last hint "that's your trouble Bob you're just practicing." Bobby just brushed the comments aside and carried on in his innocence, the three of us however kept giggling like little school children.

When we arrived at the park most of the other players were already there kicking a ball around and generally warming up but Sue and Rita had not put in an appearance yet but then I did say that Bobby wanted to see her after training so as of now I didn't think it was worth breaking the good news to Bobby that he had a date.

A Life on the Lane

After kicking a ball around and banging a few shots at Bobby for a few minutes the booming voice of the manager shattered the relative quiet of twelve or so teenage boys having fun with footballs. The manager was quite a small man but clearly very fit and he had a bit of a swagger that said "I'm the boss, do what I say when I say and I will accept no arguments" - the other thing was he looked somewhat familiar - I had thought that the first time I saw him. "Ere Fred, I was going to ask you on Sunday, do I know the manager he looks really familiar?" "You call yourself a Rangers fan, its John Collison, and you must remember him he had a bloody good career down the Bush but gave up playing with injury problems." Freddy was a die-hard QPR fan and could probably name every player that had ever turned out for them and if you asked nicely would let you know their inside leg measurements just to make it interesting.

"Right you lot, you've had your fun now let's get down to some work, two circuits of the park running except you Mark." The manager pointed at me which of course made me look round to see who had walked up behind me, "it's no good looking behind you it's you I'm talking to." "It's Malc not Mark" I responded, "well what-ever, wait for this lot to get going and then when they get to the bottom corner you can start but...." - the manager paused and looked me up and down - "I don't expect you to be the last one to finish, I've been told you are a bit of a striker and strikers need to be quick so you have got a bit of catching up to do." The boss turned to the others and shouted "well don't just stand around you lot get going." When they had set off John turned to me and with a smile quipped, "by the way when I say don't be last that doesn't include Bobby he's the goal keeper so he doesn't need to be too quick, which is a bit of luck." I watched as the team ran off along the perimeter of the park and sure enough within a few seconds Bobby was "Tail end Charlie" and again the boss looked around at me and laughed - "see what I mean, now Mark when they get to that bottom corner you go." "Malc" I said, John looked at me "what?" "My name is Malc not Mark." "Well son it's not worth learning your name because you haven't done your running yet and I have a feeling you are going to be coming back here last, with the exception of Bobby that is, but as I say he doesn't count."

I followed the progress of the others and was ready to go as soon as they reached the bottom corner, if I was going to catch the group I really needed to fly but the boss was watching "hang on you've got to wait until the last one makes the bottom corner .. And my guess is that will be Bobby." "But you said he doesn't count." "No Mark he doesn't count in the result but he does in the process."

Bobby finally made the bottom corner and that was it, I was off I ran full tilt towards the first corner and looked across the park; the leading group were in the meantime arriving at the third corner. I ran my heart out and was making progress by the time I had got one circuit under my belt but I was starting to feel the effort, my chest felt fit to burst but I really wanted to do this, I wanted to be part of a team again. As I run past the boss I couldn't tell whether he knew I was there, he was shouting at Bobby who by this time was only a few seconds in front of me, but because I was flat out and he was cruising I didn't seem to be catching as fast as I had been. I finally caught and overtook Bobby along the bottom length of the park but I knew I didn't have any chance of catching the others at this pace; in fact I needed to speed up and speed up

A Life on the Lane

a lot. Just as I was going to give up I started for some unknown reason to think about the army, Eric and PC Richard had both told me about the route marches and training and how hard being a part of that team would be but they had both said that when I put my mind to something I could do anything. "Come on Malc" I shouted out loud "I can do this" and I seemed to get a second breathe from somewhere.

As I passed the last corner I had only the home straight to go and an old man walking a little dog laughed as I approached "go on youngster the one behind is catching up." Bloody hell I thought the one behind is Bobby so I took a swift look back but Bobby was way back, I looked forward again and the leading pack seemed closer than ever with just fifty yards to go, I knew now I could do this, I had faith in my abilities it was just a case of one last push.

As we approached the boss I was within inches of the last player, this was it I thought so near yet so far, and with a half trip and half dive I went head first past the boss.

"Well done Malc" John said looking down at the heap on the floor, "I've got to say I didn't think you would do it but that last section you really did fly." I caught my breath and looked up "well boss if that old man hadn't ribbed me about Bobby catching up I wouldn't have done it I can tell you". The boss turned and looked around "what old man" "the one over there with the little dog." I looked around and sure enough there was no old man and no dog. I have no idea where he went, I hadn't noticed him arrive and certainly didn't see him go but whoever he was without him I would definitely not have got back as quick as I did and maybe even Bobby would have beaten me.

The boss carried on with the training session , there was all sorts of things to do but to round the night off we were going to get the chance to play a couple of games of one touch. One touch is fast and you need to be able to pass, shoot and think on the move, it's a five aside game but as the name implies you get one touch of the ball then you have to off load it. It was a good game for me because I was fast and could pass and shoot with relative accuracy, that was before I noticed Sue and Rita arrive. I couldn't help but look over to the side of the pitch and it seemed to be every time the ball came my way, I looked an absolute idiot nothing was working and at this rate my career in this football team was over before it had started. I had to get off the pitch and soon, I thought about it for a few minutes and just wandered over to John. "Excuse me Mr. Collison, I know this looks a bit bad but can I sit this one out, I put everything into the run and training earlier, and well to put it mildly I ain't at peak fitness at the moment," "ok Mark but if I don't see what you can do how can I think about a place on the team, Joe you get on in place of Mark here." "Thanks boss and its still Malc" I responded. I turned and walked over to Sue who was clearly as excited as me "hello Malc" Rita almost echoed Sue - "yeah hello girls, Bobby will be glad to see you could make it, I know he's been looking forward to it" I quipped. Sue and Rita looked at me and again in perfect harmony replied "well he would have been if he had known." "Oh I take it from that remark that you've already spoken to Bobby then." The two girls were beginning to sound like a double act, their reply came immediately and with faultless timing, "Bobby was the last to know Malc." "Listen Rita, Bobby's got "the hots" for you but he ain't so good at doing the arrangement bit, so I just wanted to help him along a bit." Rita was the first in with a reply, "oh so it had nothing to do with you wanting to see

A Life on the Lane

Sue again then?" "Well It's always nice to see the pair of you and I thought if you and Bobby were getting on OK Sue would make some good company for me, I just didn't want to get lonely on the way back"; "umm" Sue looked at me knowingly and fortunately for me was still smiling.

"Anyway girls I need to get back on the pitch if I'm going to get a place in this team, so can I assume that Bobby and I could have some company on the way home?" Sue looked into my eyes and the glint was really bright, she answered for the pair of them, "well Malc I sincerely hope so because we would not be happy walking out without male escorts." Sue giggled which was so attractive and with that I went back over to speak to the boss.

"Mr Collison any chance of getting back on now, I just needed a couple of minutes to get my breath back?"

Mr Collison sneered a little and called off one of the other kids, "well go on Mark get on and let me see what you can do." I didn't need telling twice I was on in the blink of an eye, I was running all over the place with my new found determination, I was in the mood to impress, I not only wanted to impress John Collison I also wanted to impress Sue. I was knocking the ball about with confidence and even managed a couple of goals. "OK lads that's it, let's call it a day I don't want you worn out before the game on Sunday. Malcolm wait a bit so I can have a word." That was a good sign I thought, Mr Collison got my name right, I waited for Bobby to make his way to the pile of clothes and stuff and let him know about his date. "What date?" "Oh didn't I tell you Rita wanted to meet you here tonight, so you might as well walk home with her and I'll keep Sue company, wait for me I've just got to talk to the boss, " and with that I ran over to

107

Mr. Collison.

"Malcolm I have to say you have got potential and yes I think I can use you in the team but as I said this is a team and we play as a team, what it isn't is the Malc show. Can you be a team member?" "Yes Mr. Collison I was brought up on team games, it's just me showing off a bit tonight and trying a bit too much to impress maybe." "OK then Malcolm see you next Sunday, I'm not saying I will play you but let's get you on the bench to start with and from now on Mark ... call me boss," and with that he sent me on my way.

CHAPTER 9
IT'S A GOOD FEELING

The first training session for a long time had came to an end and boy did I know all about it, but tonight was easy I knew the aches and pains would be at their peak in a few hours after a good night's sleep but in the meantime I had to get Sue and Rita back home. I say I had to get them home but of course Bobby was more than willing to lend a hand and escort Rita who fortunately lived just off Lancaster Road. Rita walked ahead with Bobby giggling and smiling and I have to say generally having a good time, I was walking slower with Sue enjoying the company but why did I feel guilty? I was having a good time, I'd had a good training session and was with a good looking girl but every so often I thought about Lin, I felt that maybe I was being disrespectful to her memory enjoying the company of her best friend. I guess that Sue got an idea of my thoughts because she just came out and asked, "are you thinking about Lin Malc?" I couldn't or should I say I wouldn't lie "yeah I am Sue, I just feel a little unfaithful being here and enjoying your company." "Stop there Malc there are two things, firstly it's been a long time and Lin would never want you to be a bloody monk and secondly all you are doing is walking home with an old friend." I hadn't thought of it that way and I hadn't thought about being turned down either, it just hadn't occurred to me that Sue might just want me to walk home with her - as a friend. I looked at Sue and that cheeky glint was in her eye, "don't you go thinking I fancy you Malcolm, like you I only came tonight to keep Rita company" both of us looked up the road at Bobby and Rita who by this time where arm in arm, "well I think they can look after themselves from here on in" I quipped, both of us giggled and Sue took hold of my arm and snuggled in a little. We carried on walking and it felt good. It not only felt good but it also felt right, I knew I had to move on and who better to move on with I thought, Sue seemed right and good for me and I would hope she felt the same.

By now we had almost reached Rita's home and she and Bobby had stopped to say goodnight before they got within sight of Rita's dad. Rita's dad was apparently very strict and would probably have removed certain parts of Bobby's anatomy had he got a sight of Bobby's attempt at what we all knew as "snogging" let alone where he was trying to put his hands. It was comical to watch the pair of them, Bobby would slide his hand up and Rita would brush it aside, not once but several times before we caught them up. "See you later", they barely broke rhythm as Sue and I passed them and we carried on up the road towards home. Bobby caught us up and carried on past us shouting back as he ran, "see you two lovebirds later" he was now intent on catching up with Freddy and Kit who had walked back via another route.

"I've enjoyed tonight Sue, and you are right we aren't doing anything wrong by being friends are we?" Sue stopped pulled my arm round so that I was facing her and put her arms around my neck, she kissed me with real feeling and it felt so very nice. I started to get that wobbly feeling again but Sue knew just when to stop put her arm back in mine and carry

A Life on the Lane

on walking.

In the next ten minutes or so we had almost reached Sue's house and were opposite my home and with a certain naivety I went to cross the road and head home but again Sue took hold of me, "come back here you, are you really thinking of letting me walk the rest of the way alone?" "Oh Sue sorry, no, that's the trouble I wasn't thinking." We both laughed and again she took the lead and again put her arms around my neck and kissed me, I could get used to this I thought to myself and after lingering for a minute or two we finished the walk to Sue's house. We enjoyed a brief goodnight and Sue climbed the steps to her front door then turned and blew a final kiss down to me before I turned and walked back home alone. I was walking on air, it was as if the whole world was on my side for once and I thought or maybe said out loud that I wanted to do this all over again.

I thought back to a word I had heard a long time ago and realised that I finally understood its true meaning. As I said the market was getting very cosmopolitan with punters and stallholders from all over the world. One particular stall holder who was nicknamed Abdul because of his Egyptian roots would always say "Maktub". It was a great word but at the time I had no idea what it meant so being inquisitive there was only one thing to do, ask. Abdul's real name was Daichi and on this occasion it seemed polite to use it, Abdul sold glassware and linen from his stall and had a great sense of humour, he had one of those infectious deep in the belly laughs that would get everyone around him laughing. Unfortunately for Abdul, Egypt didn't have the best dentists and virtually all of his front teeth had gone, it was something that made his laughter even more infectious, he was a real sight when in full guffaw mode. Anyway as I was saying Abdul would say Maktub at the drop of a hat but no one knew what it meant, on this particular occasion Abdul dropped a glass dish while passing it to a punter smashing loudly on the edge of the curb. Abdul wrapped another dish and this time safely passed it to the old girl and took the one and sixpence payment. Having closed the deal he went customer side of the stall to clear the broken glass moaning about his loss of the "one and six" all the time until that is the infamous word bellowed out from under the stall - "Maktub". I had heard it lots of times before but I wanted to know what had happened under the stall to elicit his reaction. Abdul emerged from under the stall grinning his broad toothless grin and again repeating at the top of his voice "Maktub."

"Daichi can I ask you something?" - "well you can ask and if I can answer I will do so little tiddler" - Abdul would never use one word when ten would do the same job. "Well Daichi what is bloody Maktub?" - Again the roaring laughter and toothless grin - "well little tiddler in my home country we follow omens and take guidance from those omens. We believe that Allah has a hand in everything that happens, for example me dropping that dish. Maktub means it was written." "Then why did you only shout it out after you got down to clean up the glass and come up with a broad smile on your boat race ?" "Ah you see little tiddler when I went down to clean the glass from the one and six dish I found a two bob bit down there, that is a tanner profit which to me is a good result out of a disaster. So breaking the dish was written and just served as a route to me finding two bob, got it?" "Yes I've got it Daichi; I think" His only response before I went back to Eric's was to laugh a deep rich belly laugh and smile from ear to ear, it was a wonderful sight.

A Life on the Lane

So why did I think Maktub as I wandered home from Sue's? Well maybe meeting up with Sue was already written and meant to be. I ran the rest of the way back home laughing as I went, even now my legs had started aching from training which just served to prove how out of condition I was.

When I got home I got Mum to run me a bath, I hadn't noticed how cold it was until now and anyway I hoped the hot soak would soften the aching muscles before morning. It's amazing how beneficial having a bath can be. That bath did me the world of good and I could have laid there for hours but dad shouted in "come on Malc, you know I've made you a cup of Ovaltine" Wow I thought it's been a long time since I had a cup of that before bed, but even tho' I thought I was a bit too grown up to be pampered like that I was glad of the treatment.

The following morning was a school day but no ordinary day because it was Thursday but no ordinary Thursday. Tomorrow was Mr. Tom's the careers master at school day and of course mum and dad had an appointment. On this Thursday morning I was up early and ready to take the bus to school but I was also up before dad had left for work. "You haven't forgotten we're seeing Mr. Tom today have you dad?" - I was just checking because I knew that he wouldn't let me down - "Malc don't worry me and mum will be there, it's important to us as well".

With the day's events sorted out the only thing left to do was get off to school, it was a bit early but there seemed no good reason to wait, I grabbed my bag and set off. I wandered off down Westbourne Park Road to the bus and to my great delight Sue was on her way to school as well. Sue went to Ladbroke Girls School but as it was only in Lancaster Road she would walk, it was just amazing our paths hadn't crossed more often. "Hi Malc you're off early, I don't normally catch a glimpse of you in the morning, but it's nice all the same." "I just kind of left early, I usually have to run for the bus but I guess today I'll get the earlier one" - "or you could walk down to the next stop with me Malc." I didn't need asking twice and Sue was clearly as eager as I was, quick as a flash she swapped hands with her bag and slid her arm in mine and as last night snuggled in a bit and again I thought this feels all right to me and we waddled off down the road.

"So what you doing today then Malc?" "Well it's a big day really; my mum and dad are coming to see our careers master this afternoon so I'm just kind of excited." "What you thinking of then Doctor, Lawyer, Stall holder?" "No the army, I'm hoping to get in the Paras." I felt Sue loosen her grip on my arm and she looked at me but the glint in her eyes wasn't there. "What's the problem Sue?" - "oh nothing Malc, it's just me being silly, it just seems like I have found you again and you're planning on leaving already, are you running away again?" - "no Sue it's not like that it just seemed that the discipline would be good for me, you know what I was like maybe I just need to do it to grow up, what is it they say give me the boy and I'll give you back the man."

Of course with all this going on I still needed to get to school and as I looked around I saw the big red Routemaster bus coming down Westbourne Park Road, "look Sue there is no way after losing myself that now I am going to lose you, it's just me, I need to do something with my life." Oh my God I thought to myself that sounds really adult and grumpy. "Look Sue can we talk tonight, I'll pop over at about 6pm if you're not doing anything." Without waiting for a reply I ran to the next stop and hopped on the number 7 bus, I grabbed the rail and looked around at Sue, she saw me looking and waved goodbye so all in all it couldn't have been all bad. I shouted back to her "see you about 6-ish then gorgeous" and ran off to the top deck. I thought to myself about last night and just how good it had felt walking back with Sue, even being with Bobby and Rita had seemed all grown up and right then I thought "no not Bobby" but again I giggled to myself and jingled the big penny pieces in my hand while I waited for the conductor to collect the fare from me.

The morning at school went pretty quick, Physics first period with Mr. Towers, which incidentally had really turned into a good subject for me, then English which was nowhere near as engrossing, after all I had learned to speak the richest language in the world and a language that was almost universal. It was a bit Roma a bit Yiddish and even a bit Jamaican with loads of Cockney so why would I now want to learn English after all I had been speaking and getting by for the whole of my life on 'market speak' good old no nonsense market talk. Anyway after the second period was a break, I must be getting above myself because "break" used to be "playtime" but for someone with a girlfriend and ambitions of an army career that didn't sound quite right so from this day forth it became break time.

The rest of the morning flew by double period of maths then lunch, the afternoon double PE and French, when was I ever going to use French I thought but of course it did keep the old grey matter working so I guess it was ok, then it was time to meet mum and dad and go over things with Mr. Toms.

I found mum and dad out by the gate in Bryony Road, being in the upper school now meant we used the smaller gate in the quieter side road. I guess that they assumed that the older kids would be more adult and respectful of local residents, and it does shock me to think they may be right, oh no was I growing up? Everything was indicating that adulthood was bearing down on me and fast.

"Hello Mum come on let's get over to the offices I expect Mr. Toms will be waiting." "Oh Malc don't worry he isn't going anywhere" mum responded and we walked past the craft workshops and round the classroom block. The office area was a separate block joined to the classrooms by a glazed lobby which was known as the foyer, which always seemed for some reason really posh to me. We went into the office block and I sought out the school secretary, "we are here to see Mr. Toms" I announced. "It's about joining the Parachute regiment". At first the poor lady looked absolutely baffled after all most of the people she dealt with were barely out of nappies and here was I announcing my intentions of becoming a leading light in the British Army.

As I had indicated Mr. Toms was a giant or at least that's how it seemed to us mortals, and indeed a giant he was even in the company of my dad. He had entered the secretary's area and with booming voice introduced himself to both my mum and dad, I however at this point seemed surplus to requirement in all the following proceedings. "Come down to the office Mr. and Mrs. Williams from what I understand your little treasure wants to join the army" and with that Mr. Toms with that usual show looked over my head and asked "is he not joining us today then?" This is getting tedious I thought but of course it was all new to my parents. "Yes Mr. Toms,

A Life on the Lane

I'm down here." Mum in particular found all this theatre interesting and actually thought it somewhat amusing, dad laughed politely but having been through this many times I chose on this occasion to ignore it which I don't think he found particularly rewarding, winding up us kids was after all a full time occupation for Mr. Toms.

The four of us went into what can only be described as the interview room and sat down, Mr. Toms behind the desk myself, mum and dad with our backs to the door awaiting the proceedings to start. Mr. Toms who had collected a folder from the school secretary on the way in took a few minutes to look over my school history, "ummm ,aah, I see" - Mr. Toms even when it was an inanimate object at the centre of his attention chose to make the most of the captive audience-. "It wasn't a particularly good start at this school was it Williams?" That lack of any title or forename led me to believe he was addressing me, "in what way?" I asked I knew as soon as I replied it was not what he wanted to hear and the fact both my parents were sitting there also made not one iota of a difference to him. He absolutely bellowed at the top of his voice. "In every way, your first couple of years were appalling, bad behavior, poor results, disgraceful time keeping shall I continue?" Mr. Toms had clearly done his homework on me but after just a brief pause he continued, "however Williams this last year or so has seen a change in you, we are obviously very good at our jobs here at this venerable seat of learning" He certainly wanted to let my parents know how good he and his colleagues were at their jobs as he continued, "you have got your head down and really made some effort, now I'm not saying you should be head boy or anything but the change WE have made in you is amazing." I just wondered at this point if I had any input into this miraculous transformation but he continued, "it's great you have turned things round Malcolm, which I have to say makes us all very proud of you." You could have knocked me down with a feather, Mr. Toms was actually saying I was becoming a star pupil, well not in so many words but it was good to get some sort of acknowledgement.

Well the meeting went on for about fifteen minutes and I had started to think my career path has yet to be addressed, "What about the army" I interjected. My question was met with silence, again - "what about my career" - my mum smiled and Mr. Toms did indeed turn the meeting around to my ambitions.

"Well Malcolm as I said at the beginning of this meeting you have started to show your full potential at last and I think that that potential needs to be given the appropriate outlet." My market brain started to kick in at this point and again I spoke up, "what does that mean, army or not?" He then to my indignation addressed my parents. "Mr. and Mrs. Williams We are of the opinion in the staff room", what has the staff room got to do with it I thought, "that Malcolm should delay his ambition of military service for a few years and take his O levels and possibly even wait and take A levels." Again I felt the need to interject, "why, why would I want to wait?" "Malcolm" Mr. Toms was now addressing me directly "as I said on several occasions you have potential, you lead, you have a good brain and we think you may have the ability to do a lot more with yourself and not just be a member of the ranks, I am not saying give up your ambitions of service but by waiting you may be able to join with the knowledge you could be fast tracked into an Officer's post, I really think you have that ability." Blimey I thought even more praise, this is unbelievable!

"I really think you should go home and consider your options with the help of your family Malcolm and if you decide to delay any decision you really could become a considerable asset for my old regiment" dad looked sideways at Mr. Toms at this point and mum smiled and added "Please Malc as Mr. Toms has said think about it we can talk at length when we get home and even run it by PC Richard." That final remark made Mr. Toms ears prick up which was also noticed by both of my parents. "It's OK Mr. Toms, PC Richard is a friend and has been guiding Malcolm through some rough times". "OK Mr. and Mrs. Williams it's agreed then if you can talk it over with Malcolm, you can always come back if you feel we need to finalise anything" and with that it appeared our careers meeting was over.

We all walked back through the school, I felt quite pleased, yes they had tried to put me off leaving school and following my ambitions but I really felt that I had been acknowledged for getting my head down, for being strong enough to get through the bad times when I had really lost the plot. Mum and dad seemed pleased too, after all they had seen what I could have become and what I could become now with theirs and the teachers guidance.

When we got back towards the car I thought that's funny where is the car, that faithful old Triumph Mayflower, which incidentally I found even then old fashioned, "where have you parked dad" "oh just down here Malc" and with that he proceeded to unlock a blue car at the side of the road. For a second I carried on walking then realised what was happening, "whose is that?" I asked and both my parents laughed. "It's our new car Malc" mum giggled that lovely little giggle of hers. "The Triumph was getting old and needed retiring so dad had been looking around for another one for some weeks and spotted this little beauty the other day, come on Malc you can ride back in the front seat if you want."

Our new car was a Renault Dauphine, which was quite unusual even rare on the roads of Notting Hill as was any car really, we had always felt lucky in that we were one of only a handful of families in our area to even have a car let alone a French exotic like the Renault. This was a peculiar car to me, for a start the cases went under the bonnet and the engine was in the boot. It had separate seats in the front unlike the only other car I had been in which had bench seats front and rear and most sporty of all the gear leaver wasn't on the steering column. Not having the gear shift on the column meant my big chance was about to happen on the drive home. "OK Malc let's give you your first driving lesson" dad said, "what - you want me to drive?" "No of course not, you're not old enough but when we get going you can learn the gears," again Mum giggled and off we went.

As we got underway dad put my hand on the gear lever and pulled the gear lever back, after a few seconds he was off again this time pushing the lever forward and to the right "that's third gear" he explained. Dad wasn't the quickest driver and anyway around the streets of Shepherd's Bush and Notting Hill which because of their nature made the journey stop start, it seemed impossible we would ever get any use out of fourth gear and sure enough with the engine working overtime we made it to All Saints Road without using more than three quarters of the available gears.

"That was good Malc; I reckon that next time you can do that

A Life on the Lane

without my hand guiding you." I thought to myself, here is my dad telling 'me', possibly the next Juan Fangio I may not need his guidance. I just thought this driving lark was child's play however with hindsight I now know that under the dash his feet where going ten to the dozen and above it his hands were turning indicators on, adjusting other bits and pieces and controlling what my hand was doing and even after all this he was still watching where we were going and what obstacles were coming our way, still as a 'know it' all teenager I knew this was going to be a doddle for me to master.

Dad parked the new car outside our front door and the three of us disembarked, one thing with dad he was a gentlemen and before he went to the front door he assisted mum out of the car and then locked it up checking each door in turn and stopping briefly to wipe a speck of dirt off the roof, mum and I looked at each other and smiled.

I knew as soon as we got indoors the conversation would have to start, the conversation about my career but in a silly sort of way I knew that actually I needed firstly to have that conversation with Sue and in my head with Linda. Sure Linda was not going to give me any advice or help but I still held her deep in my heart. It is the same whenever I get decisions to make I can only make those decisions after I have been through things in my head with her, just reassuring myself that whatever decisions I make are the right ones and would have been right if Linda had still been around.

I was quite right about the conversation I had no sooner got into the flat than mum started, "well Malc what are you thinking of doing?" I decided the best thing at this time was to just say whatever my parents wanted to hear, which I had interpreted as being to stay on at school and put the military career on hold at least for today that is. Mum must have anticipated what I was going to do because she was the one that came up with an answer that suited me and her for a while at least. "Look Malc it's probably better no one makes any decisions at this time, as we told Mr. Toms, PC Richard has been involved in this for a long time now so maybe we should run it by him first. Well Malc is that OK with you?" "Yeah that's fine mum, I have to say that I am confused, this is not how I had planned things out but then that's probably because I hadn't thought things through properly"

By now Dad had entered the room and in his usual calm way agreed with everything, "yep let's sleep on things tonight get PC Richard in and go from there." Great I thought all sorted, well for now anyway and of course I still had Sue to talk to and later on tonight in the still of my bed I had to talk to Linda.

A Life on the Lane

CHAPTER 10
YOUNG LOVE

At about 6 o'clock I made my way over to Sue's house, it wasn't far but the few minutes it took gave me more than enough time for my heart to start racing, it was becoming common place now but the "wobbly" feeling came back again and started to peak as I climbed Sue's stairs. Sue had been watching out of her window so I didn't need to knock, she made it down the stairs to her front door before I could. This is good I thought she is as eager to see me as I was to see her. "Let's go for a walk" it didn't sound like a request more like an order but it was fine with me it would be nice just to walk alone with her like we had the night before and even briefly that morning.

Sue grabbed my arm and we descended to the street and walked up the road. "Malc I'm sorry about this morning, it just took me by surprise, I have been thinking about it all day." "Oh Sue it wasn't a problem and anyway I think decisions have been made for me." Sue stopped and looked me in the eye. "What do you mean?" Without thinking I had made up my mind, I felt Linda had guided me so this was good. "Well the school seems to think I have potential and a good brain so we have decided that staying at school for a few more years and taking my exams would be a good idea" this was like déjà-vu, Sue snuggled in to me and we walked slowly on. Sue and I just kind of drifted off down the road, arm in arm like an old married couple, everything was right on planet Malc and my head was in a good place. "Fancy a cup of tea" I asked Sue, "I am sure the cafe is still open." It was funny doing these sort of things with a girl, up until now all my time was spent with the lads and we would never have dreamed about sitting in a cafe with a cup of tea, Notting Hill always had too many things to occupy us and those things were usually very loud, energetic or bordering on illegal.

Sure enough when we got to the cafe it was still open, the stallholders had finished packing up and were probably on their way home for their teas. When we went in to my surprise Nora was behind the counter, "hello Malc" she piped up "what can I get you but you had better make it quick we will be closing soon," Nora looked up again and saw Sue, "Oh hello Sue what you doing with this scallywag ?" "Oh he's not a bad lad Nora, in fact he's alright" "you two an item now then?" Nora asked Sue. That made me look up, I wondered how Sue would answer, in this whirlwind relationship I hadn't really thought about it as a relationship and what's more I hadn't actually asked Sue to go out with me, in fact quite the opposite really, I had actually said we were just friends. Sue answered Nora's query "no we're just friends Nora..." At which point I surprised even myself "actually Nora, yes we are an item." Sue looked at me with a really cheeky glint in her eyes and quipped "oye don't go getting ideas Malc we're just friends and don't you forget it." Nora put 2 cups of tea on the counter and laughed "there's your tea Malc are you two friends sharing a table?" Nora looked at Sue and remarked "He really does think he's God's gift doesn't he" Sue laughed and we went and sat down.

" Sue I know we agreed to be friends last night but since we are, well walking out a bit do you want to make it something more

A Life on the Lane

than friends ?" Again Sue laughed, "Malc I know it was forward of me but I just kind of thought we were more than just friends anyway but I am really glad you asked, yes Malc definitely more than friends."

After chatting for a while Nora called over "haven't you got homes to go to we're shutting up now?" Sue and I finished our tea and stood up and again Nora spoke up," I hope you two weren't going to run off without paying." I had completely forgotten about paying and what's more when I dipped in my pocket I was flabbergasted to realise I hadn't actually got any money. "Oh" my shocked look was a picture I'm sure but Nora took pity "don't worry Malc I can treat you two this time and anyway I was about to throw those dregs away from the pot." Sue and Nora smiled at each other "I don't know first date with me and you're penniless, I don't know that's not a good start is it?" Sue took me by the arm and we left the cafe and toddled off up the Lane.

I love this road it really is the heart and soul of Notting Hill, Portobello Road or the Lane as we locals know it is the hub, as with this evening, it doesn't seem to matter where you are going to or coming from you just seem to end up there. Sue and I carried on walking up the lane to Lonsdale Road at which point we turned left and found ourselves outside Colville School. It really did look majestic, standing there so very tall with its red brick facade and large windows, but I also remember how daunting it had looked and felt during the first few weeks there as a pupil and I realised that I had not been back past it since leaving for Christopher Wren. "Does it remind you of Lin Malc?" Sue asked. "It does but not in a bad way after all we were all so happy here, and apart from Mrs. Love giving me a clip round the ear now and then I just remember all the happy laughter." Sue

125

snuggled into me and we walked on. It didn't seem to take more than a few minutes and we had walked to Sue's house. We sat on the bottom step and talked and as "an item" I took this opportunity to steal a kiss or two as we sat there. "Fancy going to the pictures Saturday?" "Yes but will you be able to afford it this time or are you friendly with the usherettes at the Odeon as well Malc?" - We both giggled.

So that was it I have now arranged our second date and although I had laughed off my financial situation Sue was right I didn't actually have any money.

Sue's mum came to the front door, "hello Malc hope you're looking after our girl" "of course I am, after all she's a very special person to me," Sue squeezed my arm, it was done with such affection and her mum had clearly seen it and the effect it had on me. I think that she had come to the door to keep an eye on us but realised we would be fine looking after each other and she slid herself back into the relative warmth of the hallway.

After sitting chatting for a while I turned and kissed Sue but it felt stronger, more feeling more, well love. I had never felt like this before, oh I know I had loved Lin but it was a younger love, it never had time to develop into the physical adult love I was beginning to feel for Sue. I kissed her again and it was the same there was a passion there and what's more it was an adult passion. Again Sue's mum came to the door I could tell she was anxious as did Sue. "I had better go in now Malc, I am sure mum's trying to tell me I need to get my homework done." Sue's mum made some murmurs about just looking out at the street but to be honest it wasn't much of an excuse. "It's OK I've got to go now anyway I've also got homework to do and

A Life on the Lane

after all I've got a date Saturday so won't be able to do it then," "oh a date Saturday Malc and who would that be with then ?" Sue's mum laughed "have you asked the lucky young lady's mother?" I could see Sue was embarrassed "well I was just about to" I quipped "Mrs. West would it be ok to take your daughter to the cinema Saturday evening?" I put on my poshest voice and gave her a little wink. I must have the gift even Sue's mum was flattered by my cheeky side. "He! he! yes of course it is Malc, you know you really are growing into a nice young man Malc" and with that she smiled and turned to go back indoors - "not too long now Susan" - and she shut the front door and left us to say goodnight.

I took the few step up to the front door with Sue and again I kissed her, a full on, arms around the neck, pulled in tight, open lipped kiss which wasn't just fleeting but was long lingering and passionate. As a bit of a beginner at this I wasn't sure how to end it and leave but as with all of this it was coming to me quite naturally maybe that's because it was all feeling so right. I pulled away but held Sue's fingers, "you'd better go in now and get that homework done" I pulled her in towards me again and I have no idea where it came from but I just sort of nibbled her lips then turned away to leave. I heard Sue draw in a breath as I went down the steps, she had obviously got the same feelings as I had, "Night Sue" I whispered up to her and with that she turned and went in doors.

I spent a quiet Friday at school working hard in class and avoiding talking about my career prospects, I don't know why but getting into conversation about the army didn't seem the best thing to do, maybe my mates would forget that the day before I was on the verge of leaving school for a military future or should I say that's what I was hoping.

When I got home I had tea and decided to finish the homework I had been unable to concentrate on Thursday evening, I had really enjoyed walking out with Sue and the kisses while we sat on the steps were filling my head making Physics and Maths homework almost impossible again.

As time went along it seemed logical that the remainder of the evening should be spent in the usual Malc way, comic, torch and falling asleep.

I had made up my mind to get up early in the morning because I hadn't forgotten my predicament in terms of finances or should I say the total lack of money. I had decided to go and see Eric at the stall as early as possible in the hope of gaining some Saturday employment and getting my finances back on track.

Saturday morning came and I was up with the lark, I was up before my mum and before my dad left for the shop, my sister of course was still in bed, Saturday was her day off. She had left school and was working for the GPO in their telephone department. Maureen was three years older than me and was always regarded as "the clever one" I had always been compared to her through infants and junior school and she was seen as Mrs. Love's star pupil, whilst I was an also ran in the brains game. In all fairness though Mrs. Love was a good teacher she only compared us in moderation, she certainly did not alienate me by overdoing the comparisons, it seemed she knew just how far to go to get the best out of me even if that meant a tap round the head now and again. As I said I had got up early to go down 'the Lane' to earn some money for the pictures and because I wanted to see Eric, even though we had

A Life on the Lane

got over all the upsets and teenage angst I didn't see Eric as much as I should, so I didn't know if he had a Saturday lad and even if he would want me to work.

After minimal hygiene efforts, morning ablutions consisted of splashing my face with water and a quick brush of the teeth when I was in a hurry, I was off. I almost ran down Westbourne Park Road turned left up the Lane and found myself at Eric's pitch within minutes. "Stone the crows Malc you shit the bed?" - Paul laughed at Eric's remarks before piping up himself - "no that ain't Malc it's a bloody mirage Eric," both of them took to laughing as they carried on preparing the stock. "He's still here Eric, what do you think he's after?" Eric turned to me and said "OK Malc what's it to be apples, oranges, a bit of veg, you know we haven't opened yet don't you?" "Come on Eric you know I'm not here for shopping I just wondered if you needed a hand today?" "You've got some front Malc I'll give you that" Eric retorted, "what you looking for then just a couple of hours?" "Well I wondered if you needed a regular Saturday lad." "Regular and you know what that means do you tiddler - yeah we could do with a Saturday boy Malc but it isn't you this time." I was really taken aback even Paul stopped what he was doing and looked first at Eric then at me, but Eric hadn't finished "we have got something for you tho' Malc, do you think you could look after a few other jobs Malc?, you could think of it as a promotion Malc" Paul's mouth had fallen open I really don't think even he knew what was going on. "Can you get the tea, prep the produce and think about serving a few customers after all you can reach the bags now Malc and you may even be tall enough to reach across the stall to pass over the purchases to the old girls now." "Umm... yeah" by now even I was aghast, Paul still had his mouth wide open - "you catching flies in that gob of yours Paul?" Eric questioned before turning to me, "well do you want it or what?" "Yeah I certainly do." "Well get going then you should have been halfway to the cafe by now." I grabbed the tea jug and got some cash from Paul's money pouch and went off merrily to the cafe. I got Stan's jug and even Mr. Patel's on the way, as always with the market things just seem to fall into place.

When I got to the cafe as usual Nora's mum was behind the counter, "morning Malc collecting the teas today are you?" "Yeah got to keep the workers in refreshments" - same as usual is it, separate bills?" Umm that made me laugh as I said everything just falls back into place, even Glad knew the routine. "I hear you're seeing young Sue, Malc. She's a nice girl; I can see you two making a really nice couple Malc," wow I thought news travels fast. Glad could see my mind was trying to work out how she knew so she giggled and responded "it's alright Malc, Nora said you were in the other night, so I just put two and two together, it's nice Malc I'm pleased for you" and with that the tea was ready and the change was laid out in separate piles ready for me. I set off to deliver the pots of Rosie and the whole thing went to plan,

Mr. Patel of course gave me the change for getting his tea and as was usual with Stan he held on to his change. "Ere's ya tea Eric, Paul come and get it" - "right Malc some things never change and if you are going to be working for me then work you will, get polishing them apples and stack them in a nice pyramid and don't forget if the pile falls down you ain't getting paid." Paul laughed "and if it stays up we'll call you "Tutan bloody Khamun" or whatever Abdul's Egyptian mate's called" - now Eric laughed.

A Life on the Lane

I thought about Sue and then started thinking out of respect I should tell Eric, after all it just seemed polite and I'm not sure I wanted him finding out from anyone else. "Ere Eric how's the apples looking?" - "yeah good, glad you haven't lost your touch." "Can I have a word in private Eric?" Paul looked up from the caulis "Christ Malc you in discussions about salary already son?" - "no Paul it's man's business, don't worry you wouldn't understand" - "you cheeky fu...." Paul stopped mid expletive and the first customer piped up "glad you controlled yourself I'm a very sensitive person I am and I ain't used to bad language." "Yeah alright Daisy, what's it to be then?" Paul carried on and served the lady and I managed to grab a word with Eric.

"Look Eric it's like this, it's been some time now since Lin and well I just wanted to let you know that I haven't forgotten her but out of respect I needed to let you know I have been seeing Sue West" - "listen Malc no one expected you to become a priest, and I know life has to go on... and anyway I already knew!" "You knew, how? Even I didn't really know until Thursday night." Well old Randal West came in the Pub last night and asked me what I thought, I told him to tell Sue to avoid you like the bloody plague." I gasped "what?" "Joking Malc, You are like a Son to me and I don't think a girl could do better for herself, you're a good lad." I pushed my chest out and felt ten feet tall, "thanks Eric that means a lot" and I turned and got on tidying up behind the stall. Eric started his patter because the market was now coming alive, the hustle and bustle that made market life what it is.

Well Saturday went by really quickly and almost before I realised it I had got the afternoon tea for a few of the stallholders, gathered a few bob and got on helping to clear away at the end of the day. I felt good and although I had popped down and helped Eric a few times previously today felt different, it felt like this was the first day of a new life, a good life and after getting a couple of dollars, which is ten shillings for the day's work and another couple of bob for collecting teas I felt it was a good days work and a good beginning.

Eric and Paul carried on packing up and Eric called out to me as I went to take some empty orange boxes to the rubbish pile, "oye tiddler you can get off home now, me and Paul ain't got a date to go on" and the pair laughed. How the bloody hell did they know? "Go on we don't want you blaming us for making you late Malc" Paul chipped in.

I dumped the orange boxes and carried on up towards Westbourne Park Road, Stan was the first, followed by Mr. Patel "enjoy your date Malc." I don't believe it I thought and as I got down near the corner even Abdul left his stall and came down to make it clear he was in on it too. Poor old Abdul he was so busy laughing he couldn't get his words out, but it was always such a pleasure to see that mouth full of ..... well nothing really when he was letting rip with that wonderful laugh of his.

When I got home mum had already started to get tea ready, dad would be in soon and of course Maureen would be off to meet one of her boyfriends or something. "What's for tea mum?" I shouted from my room, "its mince Malc, why you in a hurry or something?" and she laughed. That's funny I thought and I headed for the kitchen followed briskly by my sister. Maureen sniffed in "crikey Malc you wearing aftershave?" she said. "No why would I be wearing aftershave?" Something's going on here I thought and then it dawned on me, they bloody know.

A Life on the Lane

"Have you two got something to say" mum just giggled but Maureen took the bait and was off. "Well Malc I've heard you might be off out this evening." I was right they all knew what was happening. "Yeah alright that's enough I'm going out with Sue." "What you going to see Malc?" mum asked - Christ they even know what I'm doing. "How do you know I'm going to pictures?" "I saw Phyllis, Sue's mum down the shop, she is really happy; it seems you made quite an impression on her." "Poor Sue" Maureen quipped. "Maureen leave him alone I think its sweet and Sue is a nice girl certainly good enough for my little soldier" mum added. "I just don't believe this, whatever happened to privacy?"

Mum served up the mince and I wolfed it down, I went back to my room to collect a jacket and of course my money after all these may be modern times, times of women's liberation etc. but I was old fashioned and I was not going to let my girlfriend pay. As I said goodbye Maureen, to my great surprise shouted after me "Malc, Malc here I've got something for you" - here we go again I thought, "yeah what is it?" "Look Malc I like Sue buy her an ice cream or something" and with that pushed a few bob in my hand.

I was so taken aback I didn't know what to say, "err thanks I will" and I toddled off down the stairs. "That was nice Mo" I heard mum say and Maureen for once had something nice to say about me, "he deserves it Mum, it's about time he was happy again."

As I got to the front door dad was on his way in "you off out - you wearing aftershave Malc?" "Don't you start" dad looked totally puzzled; actually I think he was the only person in London W11 that didn't know I was going out.

When I got to Sue's she as before was looking out of the window and as I got to the top step the door opened, but it wasn't Sue but her brother Brian. Brian was a big lad and had a bit of a reputation around the area, he was only a couple of years older than me but those two years put him in a totally different league to me. "Oye Williams you make sure you look after my sister or we might need to have words," Sue's mum had also come to the door by now and had heard Brian, "you mind your own business Brian, Malc's a good boy and I won't have you upsetting him, now bugger off you great oaf." I had never seen Brian slink off before but it made me smile inside and by now of course Sue had also got to the front door, "come on Malc lets go, what's on at the Odeon?" Sue's mum waved us off with the usual, "have a good time and behave yourself." Sue's mum also threw in a common old warning to Sue, "and keep your hand on your ha'penny." Sue went as red as a beetroot, "Oh Mum," she drew in a breath and we were off.

We walked off up Westbourne Park Road and waited at the bus stop for a number 7 bus. "This is nice Malc, just you and me, I've got to say I'm no expert on going on dates, in fact this is my first." "Well that's good" I replied "it's my first too" and Sue took my arm. As we waited we sat on the garden wall behind us and Sue snuggled in nice and close but the peace didn't last long. "Oh god no" "what's up Malc?" asked Sue. "Look its bloody Freddy and Bobby" - the two of them crossed the road when they saw us. "You waiting for a bus Malc?" As I have said before Bobby wasn't the sharpest tool in the box, here we were waiting by a bus stop what else would we be doing? "Yes Bobby waiting for the number 28." Bobby laughed, "well you will have to wait a long time this is the number 7 route 28's don't stop here." Freddy shoved Bobby "come on you dope leave them

A Life on the Lane

alone let's get off up the flicks, you know you can't wait to see Snow White." "Oh no it's not Snow White is it, I've seen that" Bobby retorted and with that the two of them waltzed off down the road holding each other's arm and pretending to be me and Sue. Sue and I laughed as they continued skipping away into the distance like Morecombe and Wise.

When the bus finally came we jumped on and headed up stairs, this time however unlike school days I guided Sue to the back seat instead of the front, in some funny way it seemed more adult. The conductor came up and collected our fares at which point Sue went to get her money out - "oh no Sue I'm paying." The clippy looked at Sue and quipped "blimey love he's a keeper that one, my old man don't pay for me" - chink, click tear and the tickets were ours, "thanks Malc you really make me feel important when I'm with you" and she kissed me gently on the cheek.

It didn't take long and we were at the cinema stop; Sue looked up at the film notice "it's Walt Disney Malc, I love Disney films," "yeah so do I but don't tell the lads I won't hear the last of it." We walked to the ticket kiosk arm in arm "two please" - "upstairs or down luv?" Upstairs in the balcony was a few pence dearer and I thought I must make a good impression but before I could answer Sue gave the response for us "downstairs please" - "oh" was my only response after all I wasn't made of money. Sue pulled out her purse but I wasn't having any of it, this was my treat and that point was not up for negotiation. I paid for the tickets and we walked to the auditorium, the usherette was standing just inside the door and I passed her our tickets. "Any seats in the back row miss?" The miserable cow looked down her nose at me and her only response was "No" and she carried on walking down the aisle. When we got about half way down she flicked on her torch and pointed to two seats halfway along the row. Oh well I thought it'll be fine at least we will be able to see the film.

We squeezed past all the other seated customers and settled into our seats; Sue rested her head on my shoulder and snuggled in close getting herself comfortable to watch the main feature. It was a good evening and after my hard day's work down the market it was really nice to just relax and even though I was tired I didn't doze off which could have been a little embarrassing to say the least.

We both enjoyed the film and left the cinema happy and content, the bus stop was heaving of course so it was Sue that suggested we walk, "yeah I'd like that" and we set off down the road with Sue snuggled in to my shoulder. "Sue I've been and seen Eric down the lane and he has given me a job, I know this sounds daft but this relationship lark seems alright to me, you are making me feel good about myself and I only hope you are happy too." "Oh Malc you do make me feel so very happy but where has all this come from?" Well I wanted to speak to your Mum and Dad." Sue looked round at me, "what? "Don't worry Sue I'm not going to ask them if we can get married or anything, I just want to ask if it's ok that you are my girlfriend, it just seems that it would be right to put US on a more formal footing after all Sue I haven't really asked you properly if you will go out with me ...... on a regular basis." Sue had a cheeky side which again I found so very attractive, she looked me straight in the eyes "go on then Mr. Williams ask!!" We both giggled - "Susan I've been thinking and just wondered if you would like to be my regular girlfriend?" Sue looked upwards and paused just a few

A Life on the Lane

seconds "ummm... yeah why not?" She was teasing me and again we giggled something we were doing a lot lately but then maybe that's how it's meant to be.

As we continued walking down Westbourne Park Road the number seven caught up with us, on the bus platform was Fred and Bobby "oye lover boy you coming to football tomorrow" Bobby shouted, they both got off the bus and waited for us to catch up. "You coming to football tomorrow Malc?" Bobby asked again. "We've got a home game and Mr. Collison was asking if you could make it, I think he might be interested in playing you, he said you might be good up front." I looked at Sue and she pre- empted me "we're not at the asking stage yet Malc you do whatever you want and anyway I could come with you and who knows we could call for Rita." Bobby laughed "too late Sue I've already asked her, she said yes by the way, seems you're not the only one with a girlfriend Malc." That made Freddy roll his eyes. "Come on Bobby I've got to get home." As I said before Freddy had duties at home, he seemed to look after his brother and sisters all the time, I knew his dad would be down the pub and his mum would have drunk a quart bottle of beer which Freddy would have been sent down to the Off License to buy before he was allowed to go out this evening and of course he would be putting the other kids to bed when he got home tonight, he was a good kid it seemed that most of his social life was on hold because of his responsibilities at home but I never once heard him complain, he just got on with it.

Freddy kicked Bobby on the backside which elicited an expected response, "oi what was that for?" "Because Bobby I've got to get home and Malc doesn't need your company at the moment so get your arse into gear will ya" and off the pair went. "They are good mates Sue" I said, "yes it's the way we are in this area" and again Sue snuggled in to me, "I feel all safe and warm when I'm snuggled into you Malc"

We carried on walking to Sue's and I sat on the stairs a few minutes, "you didn't answer Sue, shall I ask your mum and dad if I can carry on seeing you...... in a ......more permanent way, like I said I'm not talking getting married or anything." "Look Malc it's up to you but honestly mum absolutely adores you and well dad loves his little girl and wouldn't be responsible for his actions if she were hurt, but he lets her make her own decisions." "I'd still like to ask anyway so maybe I could pop round after football tomorrow." "Yeah OK Malc I'll let mum and dad know and about tomorrow you picking me up then?" - "yeah why not I'll call for you at 9 am then we can wander down to the others." Sue and I pulled each other in and we kissed goodnight, it felt good, it was, even for teenagers passionate and heartfelt, there was an intimacy that was growing and feelings that felt so grown up and good. These were feelings, passions and emotions I never wanted to be without again.

A Life on the Lane

CHAPTER 11
GETTING FORMAL

Sunday morning came and I was up early, washed and dressed with my kit ready for football and heart ready for Sue.

"Going to football Malc?" mum asked from the kitchen. " Yeah I might get a bit of a game today." "You'll be back for dinner or shall I put it in the oven?" Blimey I thought I've never been asked that before, I was always told what time I would be back for dinner. "Well it's a ten o'clock kick off so ninety minute game and fifteen minute half time then forty five minutes or so to get back... what times that ," I questioned. "Oh look if you're back good if not I'll keep it warm" - "thanks mum, got to go the lads will be waiting." "The lads Malc..?" - "bye mum"

I ran over to Sue's with my duffle bag to find her there waiting for me. Sue walked towards me and we kissed "good morning Malc." "Wow" I thought, "I spoke to my mum and dad and they.....mum said she would love to see you so why don't you pop in after the game?" Ideal I thought but I was now starting to get worried, this was going to be a frightening thing to do and I wondered why I had even mentioned it in the first place. This was the first time I had ever gone to officially meet a girlfriend's parents. With Lin of course I had grown up with her and had always known her mum and dad so this situation never arose.

139

I had known Sue's family all my life too but that was different. "Yep that's fine after football then" and with that we wandered off to Clydesdale House to pick up Freddy and Kit, Bobby was going to pick up Rita so would have left already.

We went straight to Freddy's flat and knocked on the door, Kit was just emerging from his flat at the same time. "Hello Malc you getting a game today?" Kit enquired, "well according to Freddy and Bobby, I made a bit of an impression and Mr. Collison thought I might make a striker," "well that would be good, you and me up front. Mr. Collison has been playing about with 4-4-2 formations lately and the other lad, umm Jesus he's that good I can't even remember his name, well to put it this way you'd walk all over him even with a blindfold on." That made me feel good and with that Freddy came out of his door, "morning lads.......... morning Sue, you look lovely this morning." "Oye watch it Fred she's with me." "Well mate it makes a change it's usually you chatting up my old dear." That brought a round of laughter from all of us and we set off to the rec.

After about five minutes of hearty walking and banter we heard a familiar call from behind, "oye ain't you lot ever going to wait for me, oh morning Sue what you doing here?" It was Bobby being Bobby. Sue looked at Bobby "well I'm here but where is Reet?" "Oh shit I was going to pick her up wasn't I? This girlfriend lark is bloody complicated" and with that Bobby ran off towards Lancaster Road. I looked at Freddy "I hope we've got another goalkeeper, he'll probably forget to come to the game." "Sue piped in "well I hope Rita's still waiting for him or there won't be anyone to remind him" that made all of us laugh.

It took us a good forty five minutes to get to 'the rec' so all the lads with the exception of Bobby were going into the changing

A Life on the Lane

room. Freddy picked out John Collison and called out to him, "ere boss I've got Malc here, we gonna try that new formation out?" John came over "Freddy, Malcolm" yeah winner I thought, at least he got my name right, "well Malcolm get changed and we will see how things are going, no promises mind." Mr. Collison walked off; Sue came over, "You playing Malc?" - "just got to wait and see, if things are going well, probably not but let's wait and see after all Bobby ain't here yet !"

I went to the changing room and got changed, "ere Malc that spotty bloke, he's our other striker and by the looks of him he didn't have his porridge this morning, Dave and Steve will drop back to midfield if you come on, sorry when you come on, the other lot won the league last season so we ain't going to get anything against them." "That's the wrong attitude Freddy; you will never win if you don't believe." With that the door flew open and Bobby came in closely followed by Mr. Collison, "get your bloody kit on Bobby it's always you, can you remember where you're playing?" - "well" responded Bobby - "you didn't say any different so I guess I'm in goal boss" the manager just turned around and left and Bobby was pelted with shoes and stuff and we all had a bloody good laugh.

When we went out Sue and Rita had sat themselves down on the halfway line, so after warming up I wandered over. "Oye Martin," Mr. Collison called over, "and where do you think you're going?" - "just over to the halfway line and its Malcolm." "Well you listen here lad as substitute your job is here near me, I tell you when you can go to see your girlfriend, this team will get nowhere without discipline, you got that?" Inside I was boiling, that was in front of the whole team and what's worse in front of Sue, I swallowed hard and just said "yes boss," Freddy looked at me in disbelief I hadn't risen to the bait, I just wandered back over close to Mr. Collison.

Mr. Collison said "listen to me Malcolm I need you to watch what's going on up front, especially keep an eye on Jerry," Jerry was the spotty kid that played upfront. "He's a bit slow up front but got potential, and the two wingers' watch them see what they do when the play is in our half, I want to drop them back to midfield and try a 4-4-2 shape." I was amazed one minute I'm being ridiculed and the next I'm assistant manager, but I would do as I was told.

Kick off came and to be fair the team did ok, they weren't winning and in fact they weren't drawing but from what I saw only three goals in the first half against us was, well bloody lucky. The lads came off the pitch and looked totally dejected, Mr. Collison gave them first a piece of orange then a tongue lashing but after a few minute again he amazed me, "Malc what did you see, how did Jerry do?" "Well to be honest John, sorry Mr. Collison, Jerry wasn't the main problem he wasn't getting any service from the wingers everything was coming up the middle and Kit had that covered as best he could." "Yeah that's what I thought" and with that he walked off. Sue and Rita had walked around to this side of the pitch, Rita had managed to get a quick cuddle out of Bobby and Sue just asked if I was going on. "I don't know Sue; it's a bloody mystery to me."

I went back over to listen to the team talk "I'm giving it ten minutes and then when they settle down I'm changing the formation" everyone looked around at Jerry but it seems the boss had other ideas. "Jerry when Malc comes on I want you to drop back to centre midfield, you will need to feed the ball to Malc and Kit alongside Steve, sorry Dave that means you coming

A Life on the Lane

off, so the back four are staying the same and the midfield from left to right is Shaun, Steve, Jerry and John you will really need to run because you'll need to cover the whole pitch getting back when necessary, now let's get those chins up" and with that they ran back onto the pitch. Mr. Collison came over to me again, "can you do the job Malc?" Crikey I thought I know he was a pro but honestly this is a Sunday league game but whatever he wants to hear I guess, "Yes boss I can cover that." Ten minutes passed and sure enough at the right moment the boss took his chance and pulled Dave off, the look I got from Dave spoke volumes, here was I just arrived and he was being substituted to let me on, but that's the nature of the game I'm afraid.

Well the good news was we didn't concede any more before Kit managed to wriggle his way through and get one back for us. All in all the second half was good and in fact had we played like that in the first half I'm sure we could have got at least a draw if not a win. I had watched QPR for years and had never really understood what they meant when they said "the manager is building a team" for this or that but just in those few minutes with John Collison he had taught me so much. He really understood formations and players potential and fit, but then I guess he should after all he made his living at it before retiring. That was it then a 3-1 loss but actually everyone thought we had achieved something, something to build on and it felt good, good to be part of a team.

The boss followed in behind us to the changing room "well lads what a great second half, I was impressed, the work rate was amazing but I'm not going to go over that today. It's a training and debriefing session on Wednesday, see you all then lads and again well done," and he turned his back to leave but as he reached the door he turned and said "one more thing that second half was good but it's down to Bobby we didn't concede anymore, that was a great performance lad" and again he turned and left. You could have knocked Bobby down with a feather but he was right I think we all understood what teamwork was and how it affects everyone's performance.

Sue and Rita were waiting outside the dressing room for Bobby and I to emerge, "Oh Bobby you were great today" cooed Rita "do you really think so, Mr. Collison said it was all down to me." I was going to point out that the boss didn't actually say that but it's not every day that Bobby gets to be proud of anything after all. Sue looked at me and quietly and privately said "Malc you were wonderful, I don't know much about football but you looked good to me." I was glad I hadn't said anything to Bobby, now I knew how he felt because I felt the same. Bobby and Rita walked off together and Freddy and Kit emerged from the dressing room, "we're going to walk on ahead lads, see you later" and with that Sue and I went off arm in arm. "Malc you in a hurry?" Sue asked. "Sorry Sue but I've got an appointment you know, I'm a bit nervous." "Oh don't be daft," that was easier said than done I thought.

It only took about thirty minutes to get back to Sue's. Well this is it I thought and we climbed the steps. Sue opened the front door and again we climbed the stairs to her flat and she called out "Mum we're back" Mrs. West emerged from the kitchen wiping her hands on a tea cloth, she was wearing a flowery pinny and had a scarf on her hair which covered her rollers, it was nothing unusual however, all the wives looked and dressed the same back then, there wasn't usually any airs and graces.

A Life on the Lane

Mrs. West giggled "nice to see you Malc, your mum and dad ok?" "Yeah fine Mrs.. W" and with that Brian emerged and just gave me a look, "see you later, don't save dinner for me, I'll get something when I'm out" and with that he slid down the banister. I looked over to Sue and without having to say anything she said "don't worry about him, he's just going through a difficult stage" - "yeah take no notice of him Malc" Sue's mum added.

I was invited into the living room where Mrs. West sat down next to her husband, that in itself was unusual, not that they didn't sit together it was just that Sunday lunchtime was a pub day so I was clearly keeping him from his pint. "Well Malc? Sue said you wanted to ask us something." I was shaking, Sue's dad hadn't said a word, he just sat there looking at me. "Umm well I ain't going to ask for your daughters hand in marriage ha! ha!" that went well I thought as not a word was uttered. "Oh mum, dad stop teasing, they know why you're here Malc, actually they are fine with it but I know you want to say it yourself so go ahead." Sue's mum and dad both smiled and Mrs. West chirped up, "go on Malc what you got to say?" "Well Mr. and Mrs. West it's like this, I know we are only young but I really wanted to ask your permission to see Sue, well as my girlfriend." Sue's mum responded, "Malc we think you are a lovely lad," Mr. West rolled his eyes, "and we would be very happy for you to, what do they say now, date our daughter." "Thanks Mrs. West but I have not been the best kid in the world of late but I really think I've changed, you know I've even got a Saturday job again." With that Mr. West stood up and spoke, "Malc we all think you're a great lad, except maybe Brian but he doesn't count, so we would be happy for you to see Sue - but don't hurt her" - and with that he left the room, he was off to get a quick pint before dinner.

Sue got up and took my hand "there, you see that wasn't too painful was it?" I smiled "no it has made me feel a lot better, I know it's daft but I just wanted to do things right." "Glad to hear it" said Sue "now let's get out from under mum's feet." - "you're not in my way love" - "I know that mum but well you know... Come on Malc lets just go and sit on the steps a while" - "ok but I can't stay too long I expect my mum will have dinner ready too."

We went and sat out on the top step but to be honest it was a bit cold and grey, Sue held my arm and we kissed, "I'm so proud of you today Malc, what with the football and then mum and dad. It really was such a lovely thought of you to ask them about us and I'm so glad you did." "Ah Sue it was a selfish thing at first, I wanted to do it for me, to try and be a better person and not make mistakes like I have in the past, but now I know that just doing things right is how you do things right for other people, people you care for" again Sue kissed me. "I like that Sue, I think I might actually be getting used to it you know, do it again just so I can make sure," and we kissed again, "yep I like that" and we laughed, I was really happy and had found a new contentment in my life.

"Sorry Sue I'd better go for my dinner now and I know you have to do homework this evening, I'll pop over sometime tomorrow," I kissed Sue yet again and went off down the steps, as I got to the pavement and started off someone called, "Malc you got a minute?" I looked round and with those big bounding steps of his PC Richard was coming along, PC Richard of course was Sergeant Richard now but he was still hands on when it was his work around our few streets and to me and my family he

A Life on the Lane

would always be PC Richard." Hello Malc, been trying to catch up with you for a couple of days now." "Why what have I done then?" "Oh don't be so defensive Malc, I heard you had been a bit tied up in other areas so I didn't pursue it too hard, anyway how you keeping, I hear your playing football again and you have a new girlfriend?" "Crikey Richard you have been checking up on me, you got my house staked out?" Richard laughed, "no! you know me though I'm a bit of a nosey bugger Malc, do you mind if I walk with you a bit ?" "Of course I didn't mind but it did sound a bit ominous I have to say. "Yeah that's fine Richard but I can't hang around too long, mum will have dinner ready." "Yes I know Malc I popped in to see your mum and dad earlier, they said I might find you around here about now, I just wanted to tell you something, come over here and sit on the wall" This was beginning to sound serious I thought. Richard and I sat on the wall surrounding Clydesdale House, "well what's all this about then?" Richard looked up and around, "Richard you're worrying me now, just get on with it will you." "Well you may take this as good news or you may feel you have been cheated but I thought you should know.... Michael is dead." I had a complete range of emotions within a few seconds, first I was elated, glad that he was gone, then the frustration that he had been living the high life for years after what he did to Lin and finally anger that we would not see him get the punishment he deserved, we had now been denied ever seeing him get his just deserts.

Richard didn't say anything further, he waited while I gathered my thoughts, and it was me that spoke first. "What happened Richard, did he suffer the way we have suffered?" "We don't know all the details Malc but needless to say he was involved in some crime of some sort back in the West Indies and the result was he lost his life and that's all I know Malc, I'm sure you will hear different things which is why I wanted to tell you personally." I couldn't help it I was not so much happy as relieved inside, some time ago Peter the Pole had died of what was said to be natural causes, but again I had felt cheated, he too had lived his time out in relative happiness compared to the many people he had hurt and used, and it was a sad thought that he had died a millionaire, a vast amount of money taken at the expense of the ordinary people of our area.

It's a shame that neither Peter or Michael had now lived to see their empires destroyed, in the interval since Peters death housing associations had taken over some of his properties; they were renovated, improved then rented out at affordable rents to local people, people that needed them and deserved to be treated with dignity and respect.

I was brought back to reality by Richard asking how I felt, "I'm fine Richard of course I'm glad he's gone and I think that now we all should forget him and get on with our lives, we know the world is a better place without him so that's it, it's one whole sorry saga over and done with." "I'm glad you're so adult about it Malc I am sure you will move on" and with that he stood up to leave. "Thanks for letting me know Richard I really do appreciate it." Richard smiled then walked away.

I sat there for a few moments and then looked up to our flat, I could just see mum looking out of the window, she must have spotted Richard and I sitting there chatting. I waved but she had moved away from the window. I knew dinner would be ready but my thoughts turned to Lin and her parents, I just felt I should go and see Eric and Jean, they should know what had happened too, so instead of going home I walked round to Lin's

A Life on the Lane

but when I got there I just stopped and looked at the front door, I had of course been back there but with the news I had just received it all came back to me just as vivid and real, it seemed like only yesterday. I turned to walk back home but didn't get more than a few yards down the road when I heard Eric call out to me, I stopped where I was and turned to face where I had heard Eric's voice come from, Eric was walking towards me, when he got to me he put his arms around me like a father does to a small child and all he said was "I've seen Richard Malc and he told me, he was looking for you." "Yes Eric he found me outside Sue's house and we chatted." "Are you OK Malc?" That was Eric all over, his concerns and thoughts were for someone else above himself. "It's all over now Malc" my only response was "yes Eric it's all over," and we both turned and walked in our respective directions.

When I got home, mum smiled, "I saw you talking with PC Richard, he came here earlier, is everything OK, you don't have to talk if you don't want to?" "Its fine mum, I'm happy now I know I will never be stumbling in to him again." My mind went back to when I had bumped into him in Tavistock Road and PC Richard had seen what was happening, he will never know but he became a hero of mine that day, he didn't need to bully, he didn't even need to raise his voice but he made it clear to me who was the bigger man and it wasn't Michael. Mum brought me back to my senses "are you eating now Malc, I've kept it warm for you?" "Yes that's fine mum and I sat down at the kitchen table."

Dad came in the kitchen "hello Malc, there's a Western on TV later you staying in to watch it?" and he whispered in my ear "I could do with the company you know what your mum thinks about Western's so she'll be happy staying out of the way doing the ironing or something," before I could answer mum asked what was going on "what you two planning, I'm guessing there's a cowboy film on this afternoon and I'm not wanted around?" Dad looked at mum and somewhat more loving than I can remember him being responded, "actually yes it is a Western but it would be nice if we all sat down together and watched it." Even mum was taken aback, "yes that would be nice and will Maureen be joining us?" Mum had seen my sister arrive at the kitchen door, "yes Maureen will be joining the rest of the family and what's more when the ice cream van stops outside, Maureen will be buying us all Ice cream even if it is cold outside." For some unknown reason my big sister was being a nice big sister again and again splashing out her hard earned wages, "but" she went on "that's only if mum irons my work clothes for tomorrow for me." Maureen smiled towards mum, she knew mum would be doing ironing later and would probably have done it for her anyway, but it was a good result all round.

Sure enough late afternoon the Tony Bros ice cream van stopped just outside our place and of course I was designated ice cream fetcher for the day, "four cones is it then?" Dad looked up and added "yes and I'll pay for the flakes." "Right that's settled then four ninety nines and no changing your minds now." I collected the money from dad and Maureen and off I scooted, you had to be quick it was four flights of stairs down and being cold not so many people wanted ice cream, which meant not so much of a reason for the ice cream man to hang around. Of course having rushed down the stairs it was the same journey back, it was a bloody good job I was fit, I thought. "Ere you go ninety nines all round" and I sat down to

A Life on the Lane

watch the rest of the film. We enjoyed the ice cream treat and as usual dad and I enjoyed the film, it was a classic Sunday afternoon, even mum and dad had snuggled up to each other on the sofa, Maureen disappeared off to her room to get ready to go out in the evening, but I really enjoyed the easy restful afternoon.

Mum got up from the sofa after the film had finished and announced that it was time for a bite to eat, "Is it that time already?" dad enquired, "well it will be soon because I've got loads of ironing to do and I don't want to be standing behind an ironing board at midnight" and with that mum left the room.

Melvin Wilkinson

CHAPTER 12
THE PRECIOUS THINGS

The following morning I made a conscious decision to get going a little earlier than usual; it was a cheeky way of seeing Sue. I had thought if I got to the bus stop early it would be nice to walk down with her to her school but of course it wasn't as obvious as waiting outside her house.

It was a rush but with a little effort I had got up early and got washed and dressed in record time, I grabbed my school bag and mum handed me dinner money, "you're early and in a hurry this morning Malc, something to do with that young lady of yours?" "Oh mum of course not" and with that I was off down stairs.

I hurried along All Saints Road turned into St Luke's Mews, I went that way so as to avoid meeting Sue before the bus stop but I was surprised at the Mews there were vans, lorries and builders all over the place. Normally I wouldn't be interested in building work in the area but this was all happening right where my secret hiding hole was. I had a bit of a panic all my precious little bits were still stashed there, the bottle top ring Lin gave me, that special little picture of her and of course the aluminium label I got at the station with dad. I know that over the last few weeks or more I hadn't been there to look at them but I got a lot of comfort from knowing they where there

152

A Life on the Lane

whenever I walked down the Mews. "Ere mate what's going on here then?" One of the builders looked round and with a deep Irish voice boomed out a response, "well by tonight this little plot of land will be cleared and tomorrow we can start building some nice posh Mews houses for the rich folks" he laughed as he turned back to his colleagues. This was a disaster I didn't know whether the wall at the back would be there when I got home from school and if it was even if I could get in to retrieve my treasured possessions, back then they still used night watchmen on building sites. I was almost in tears as I walked on down the Mews; I turned left on Basing Street and continued on to Westbourne Park Road, as I got to the bus stop Sue was just getting there too. "Morning Malc, early again aren't you?" - "yeah just a bit, I was awake so just got on with getting off to school." "Come on then Malc lets go, you can walk me down to school."

Sue grabbed my arm and off we went but I didn't really engage in much conversation. "You OK Malc?" Sue enquired, "yeah yeah fine." "No you're not Malc what's up?" I was reluctant to answer after all it was all about Lin and I had only just started seeing Sue properly. "Malc come on I know there's something wrong please tell me." "Well Sue don't get angry or upset but it's to do with Lin." "Malc I won't get angry but please tell me." I knew I was backed into a corner and had to tell, "this will sound really daft but they're building in St Luke's Mews." "So what has that to do with you or Lin?" "Well Sue when I was really young I had a special place that I hid special things....." - Sue interrupted, "what special things?" "Well silly things really, there is a photo of Lin and well, sorry Sue, but a ring that she gave me, you know we always thought we would be together forever and that ring was our way of being sort of engaged

I guess." Sue tugged my arm and turned me around, so that I was looking back up the road the way we had just come. "You angry Sue?" "Yes a little Malc - but not because you have stuff hidden but because you did nothing to retrieve it, come on if you won't get it I will" Sue answered, "but you will be late for school" - "move Malcolm and that's an order." I didn't think there was any point arguing it seems Sue had made up her mind.

When we arrived at the Mews the builders were still standing about chatting, Sue marched straight up to them and simply asked if she could retrieve a ball that had been lost over her garden wall the day before, and she pointed to the back wall of the site. The builders looked around looked us up and down and just said "go on then but hurry up the machines will be here to clear the site soon." Bloody hell I thought that was easy and we went over the back wall. Sue pretended to look for the ball while I retrieved all my stuff from behind the loose brick. "You got it Malc?" - "yep all of it." "OK let's go then" and we went back towards the roadway. "Found your ball missy?" enquired the big Irishman. "No never mind" responded Sue "but if you come across it throw it back in my garden will you, it's that one there" and Sue pointed towards one of the houses. I of course knew that Sue lived nowhere near those houses and we walked off again down the Mews. "Sue that was genius." "I can't believe you didn't think of something like that yourself Malc, you're the one that is supposed to be all streetwise and crafty," we both laughed as we walked on arm in arm. Sue and I walked all the way to her school entrance and watched as my bus went by, "now who's going to be late for school Malc?" "Well I guess it's going to be me Sue, but never mind it doesn't happen much these days, I'll be OK."

A Life on the Lane

Sue kissed me tenderly and pushed me off on my journey to school, "thanks Sue, you really are special, I'm not sure I deserve you" - "go on get off to school you soft bugger."

As I've said many times before school was being good for me these days to the point I actually enjoy going, Sue didn't need to tell me twice but today I was late....very late. , never mind I thought it's worth missing a little schooling to be with Sue for that extra 5 minutes.

I carried on walking to school in fact I didn't wait for a bus, I just jogged all the way and took the time to think up an excuse for my form master. When I finally arrived at school I was about a half an hour late and I couldn't believe it, who was waiting at the gate checking on late comers and early leavers but Mr. Toms. "Aah! Williams good job I happened to be looking at the waste paper down there or you might have slipped in under my nose. So now enlighten me what caused this little hiccup Mr. Williams.... death or ill health in the family..?" I thought I would stop him there - "no....." "Let me save you from lying now" interjected Mr. Toms, "if it was your grandmother again it's the third time she has died perhaps they should cremate her this time just to make sure Williams." "That was very funny Mr. Toms, Sir" I replied "that's why you are my favourite master, clever, a great teacher and so funny, but no it was nothing like that I just overslept and that led to missing the bus and a long jog to school, I'm very sorry sir." "Oh said Mr. Toms, well it's quite rare these days so I guess I can overlook it this time.... off to class now Malcolm." Crikey I thought he is getting soft, no detention no reporting to the headmaster and to top it all he called me Malcolm, result.

155

By now the first period was coming to an end so I found my form master and let him know that he needed to amend the register. "That's easy enough I haven't taken it to the office yet Malcolm consider it done, but who was on the gate this morning?" - "oh it was Mr. Toms, I explained why I was late and he just told me to get to class." "Really" he replied in a mystified voice," you'd better do what he said then" so off I went.

The school day came to a close nothing really happened it was just another day, a day like most others. It was just another mile along life's wiggly road.

A Life on the Lane

CHAPTER 13
CHANGES

I had grown up a lot over the past few years not only in size but also in my brain box, I felt I understood more of how life worked, and I did of course know an awful lot about what the world could throw at you. I knew both physical and mental pain and in the end I guess I learnt how to cope with it. Now was a time I was also learning about changes in circumstances, my dad having left the army after the war had trained as a butcher, it had been his job for many years but for some reason he was now getting restless and wanted to move on. Maybe it was a lot of what was happening around us and he felt that perhaps now was a good time to really ring the changes.

Just prior to this my dad had been manager of a Co-op butchers shop in Shepherd's Bush which was just a stone's throw from my maternal grandfather's house. Grandad had been on his own for some time since my Nan had passed away and dad had now taken it on himself to go in for his dinner on a daily basis to keep an eye on him. Grandad always liked my dad and now with his daily visits who knows what they talked about, but what I do know is that the bond they had was growing stronger. Dad had always called him "the Governor" and I had only just realised exactly how much respect this was meant to bestow on him.

As with most people that suffered the war they rarely spoke of the horrors, Grandad during the First World War and dad the Second. It was on a rare visit with my mum that I actually sat down with Grandad, I say rare because of late I just hadn't had the time. For some unknown reason he opened up to me. I wondered why me, he had always been much closer to my sister but on this occasion whilst mum was upstairs cleaning he got out some dusty old magazines about the battles of WW1, as he flicked through the dog eared pages he spoke in a low melancholy voice. It seemed that at every page turn he remembered someone that was killed, maybe it's the passage of time but I swear he had a tear in his eyes. I had never guessed that he had gone through so much and lost so many people that had been so close to him. I wasn't sure if this was meant as some kind of warning to me or that he just needed to get it off his chest, what I did realise was that his experiences had created a bond with my dad and now myself, maybe it was something to be passed down the male family line, who knows?

A few weeks later we as a family had quite a shock, dad had visited 'the governor' for his lunch and had found him on the floor of his kitchen. My mum got a call and she made her way over to Shepherd's Bush calling in to pick me up from school. "Malc I've got some bad news" she said, she had a tear in her eye, it's grandad, dad's at his house now" - "what's happened mum, tell me what's happened." "Grandad's died son." It may seem a bit crass now but I just said "is he alright?" "No Malc he has died." "Sorry Mum I meant Dad, he will be devastated, and you need to look after him." Mum just put a hanky to her eyes and wiped away a tear, how stupid was I, she just got news that her dad had passed away and I was asking her about my dad. She spoke to me like an adult and as usual her kind and feeling words made all the difference. "It will be hard for him and all of

A Life on the Lane

us but we will all have each other to lean on," and with that we walked off towards Thorpebank Road where 'the Governor' lived.

As we walked down towards his house my mum put her arm round my shoulder and smiled, "when I was young and had started seeing your dad I lived here" she said, "there are so many happy memories." As we got closer mum said "can you see what is different between grandad's house and all the rest Malc," we stopped and I gazed at the fronts of the terrace of identical houses. "No mum they're all the same." "No they aren't, look above the door porch" and then I noticed grandad's house was the only one without a finial on the apex of the porch. "It was at the beginning of the war and I wanted to go out, but your grandad would have none of it, we had such an argument and he made me go to my room." "What's that got to do with the finial on the porch?" I asked. "Well don't be impatient I'm coming to that, you take after me more than you know Malc, I knocked that finial off climbing out of my bedroom window, similar to what you would probably do." I laughed I'm not actually sure that even now at my age I really would have the bottle to defy my mum and dad like that but then of course my bedroom window was three stories up with no porch to climb onto.

As we went in the kitchen door was closed and dad was sitting in the front room smoking. He stood and hugged mum and me in turn. "Have you told Mo yet?" he enquired. "No I phoned Brian and he is going to meet her from work." Brian was Maureen's long term boyfriend, well when I say long-term it was only a matter of weeks but he worked close to Maureen's so could get there easily to meet her.

159

I really didn't have anything else to do with the rest of the proceedings it was all down to mum, dad said the doctor had been, and in my naivety I just thought, what good is a doctor. "We are just waiting now for the undertaker to collect him there will of course be an autopsy" dad said and mum hugged him and sent him back to work to close the shop.

Sure enough in the fullness of time someone came to collect grandad and I was left in the front room as he was removed, I couldn't help it I had to look out of the window as he left. It wasn't long after he was taken that mum came back into the front room and she just held me, I looked into her eyes and asked, "will they bring him home before the funeral mum?. I think I would like to say goodbye and have a private word with him" Mum smiled, "of course they will Malc, we need to tell uncle Bill and other members of the family that want to see him, so he will be brought home the night before so that we can see him," and again she had a little tear in her eye.

Dad came back to pick us up and take us home and I guess that was it really nothing else I could do but go home, I needed to go and see Sue, funny because yes I needed to see her, I wanted to tell someone what was in my head and I wanted it to be Sue. Is that being a little bit disloyal to my family I thought but that's how it was, I needed to talk to her for me, OK disloyal and selfish maybe.

When we got home Maureen was already there, she was devastated and being a daddy's girl he put his arm around her and whispered something which seemed to help, but it was as if Dad had taken her pain and added it to his own, it was now him that was showing signs of tears. "I've got to go and see Sue Mum, don't do me anything to eat I'm not hungry." "Malc I

A Life on the Lane

hadn't even thought about cooking and I really am not feeling like eating, so you go to Sue's." Mo had got the same idea as me and had decided to go to Brian's which to my way of thinking was a good idea it left mum and dad alone to talk and mourn a little.

I ran to Sue's like my life depended on it and it was only a matter of 1 or 2 minutes before I was climbing her front steps. I rang her door bell and within a few seconds her mum answered "oh hello Malc where you been Sue's doing some homework then getting ready for bed, she was expecting you earlier." "I'm sorry" I blurted out" but my grandad died." "Oh I'm sorry" said Mrs. West "I'll get her but she can't be out long," and with that she pinched my cheek and went for Sue. Why do adults do that I wondered, it bloody hurts for a start, oh well I thought grownups will be grownups I suppose. Sue came running down stairs and leapt into my arms, I'm not sure her feet touched the ground between me and the bottom step but I do know it felt so good to know how much we meant to each other. We really had grown a relationship so quickly and many of the things that break up lesser couples simply made our love stronger, did I say love well yes maybe it was love?

" You ok Malc, mum told me, hope your mum and dad are ok too" - "yeah we're all fine just a bit of a shock really."

Sue hugged me close and kissed me, for once she didn't seem to care that her mum or dad could come out and catch us. I was just so comfortable, she kissed me for what seemed forever and I had no reason to pull away. This really was passionate I thought, her tongue probed my mouth and I felt that old wobbly feeling again. I had of course kissed like this before but for the first time it really did have feeling and meant so much.

When we broke I went quiet, I think that it was the feeling and passion that had passed between us and the fact I wanted to ask Sue a favour which now felt a little, well and at the risk of repeating myself, just a little disloyal. It had been some time since Sue and I had retrieved my special stuff and to be honest I had either been carrying it around or tucking it away in my sock drawer, I wanted Sue to look after it, should I dare ask now?

As usual Sue knew me better than I knew myself, "why you gone quiet Malc, have I upset you?" "No of course not, I wanted to ask you something but your kiss just took my breath away.......wow" - "come on then ask." "Well Sue you know those little bits and pieces we retrieved from the wall down the Mews," "yeah Lin's stuff" - "yes well I don't really know what to do with them, it's only the ring and the picture really, so...." Sue interrupted, "of course I will Malc, I'll put them with my special bits" again Sue knew almost before me what I was going to ask, it was that telepathic thing we seemed to have going between us.

Sue promised to store my stuff in her jewellery box, I had seen it before and looking back now it was so 1960's. Her jewellery box was a classic it was white wood and when you lifted the lid a little ballerina popped up and pirouetted. It's strange but I remember Lin had one the same, as I said they were a cliché of the 60's and 70's and I would lay money that they came from a stall down the Lane.

"Do you want to talk about your grandad Malc?" Sue asked. "No not really Sue but can we have a quiet time on Saturday, you can pop over to my place after I finish work if you want." I think as part of the growing up phase of my life my parents allowed certain goalposts to be moved, it hadn't really been

A Life on the Lane

acceptable to take girls back to my bedroom but now with Sue we got a bit more freedom. This freedom did come with a warning though, I can still hear my mum now, "don't get up to any hanky panky Malc, Sue's a nice girl, and don't forget I can pop in any time to check up" then she'd laugh and add, "you're a chip off your father's block so don't forget I can still remember what he was like when we were courting....." "Oh don't mum that's disgusting...!!" was always my stock reply to anything involving any type of passion between adults and especially my parents, after all I was found under a gooseberry bush, wasn't I.....?

Sue and I sat down on the bottom stair in the hallway and chatted, we talked about schoolwork, football and anything else that came up but Sue had an understanding and didn't mention my grandad or Lin, after an hour or so during which time Sue's mum or dad didn't come out once, I felt it was time to say goodnight. I stood up, "I'm going now Sue but don't forget Saturday." Sue stood up "of course I won't silly, I'll be there" and inside I knew she would. She pulled me in gave me another of those wonderful kisses, for once it was me that pulled her in closer to me, I rubbed my hands down her back and then just brushed them over her breasts. It was me that pulled back, "I'm sorry Sue that was wrong." Sue looked me in the eyes and smiled, "did I say anything Malc?" "No but it wasn't right." "Shut up you daft sod give me a kiss then off you go," I smiled and did exactly what I was told.

I opened the front door and went down the steps. I turned and said goodnight and Sue responded "goodnight Malc... I love you." I smiled without realising what she had said and started to go off down the road. I turned and went back and tapped on the door hoping Sue hadn't got back upstairs. "It's me I forgot something," the door opened immediately, Sue hadn't even started to go to her flat she was just standing with her back against the door smiling. "I know Malc your special stuff." I dipped into my pocket and found the photo and bottle top ring and handed them to Sue, "and I forgot to say, I love you too Susan West," and I turned again descended the steps and ran off down the road as Sue closed the door. As I ran I repeated Sue's words ... "I love you" "wow she loves Me, Me wow" I'm not sure any of that makes sense but that's just how it goes, wobbly feelings, jumbled up words and not knowing what day it is, there you have it that's the Malc Williams definition of love.

Saturday came around and mum had been running around doing stuff concerned with grandad's death, back in those days not everyone had a phone at home so it meant relying on someone local that did have one or using the public phone. Mum tended to use the phone box on Talbot Road, I still have no idea how many calls she made but she seemed to be going to the phone box continually.

I of course had to go to work with Eric, work was still my haven and it was never a chore getting up and working with Eric and Paul. Paul and Eric had been a team for as long as I can remember, quite literally, from my earliest memory Paul had been there, I never really knew much about him he was a private man which in our environment was unusual. Paul it turned out was an orphan that's as much as I know and that only came out when we spoke about 'the Governor'.

"'Ere Malc, sorry to hear about your grandad" Paul blurted out, "I ain't got anyone that close" he said. "I was brought up in a home, an orphanage, but I know how you must be feeling." "Thanks Paul I appreciate that," and that was the end of the

A Life on the Lane

conversation really. I wasn't sure if Paul regretted not having someone to lose or if he was grateful but either way that was Paul's lot and on the whole I think he was happy with his life. The day went on and as it drew to a close I started thinking about Sue, I thought about what we had talked about and wondered if she meant what she had said. Again I felt a bit disloyal doubting her, I had no reason to. Sue was the most loyal and honest person I knew or could ever know. Eric brought me back with a jolt, "oye tiddler" I hadn't heard that in a while, "you bloody day dreaming lad, cos I don't pay you to day dream." "Sorry Eric yeah I was, I was miles away, and we've had some good times on the market haven't we. It's a part of my life that means so much to me." I walked over closer to Eric, "I owe you an awful lot, I couldn't wish for a better friend, thanks." "What the bloody hell brought that on Malc, you thinking about your grandad?" "Yeah a bit and sorry for day dreaming Eric," "don't worry son I was only kidding you, look, you pick the rubbish and take it up to the dump then you can get off." I didn't need telling twice, I was diving here there and everywhere picking up boxes and other rubbish, under the stall, in front of the stall and behind the stall. I was darting about so much Paul had to tell me to get out from under his feet. "Alright boss this is the last lot now, I'll put it up at the dump and get off." "OK Malc, have a good weekend" and off I scampered.

I had been to the dump and came back past the stall and to my surprise PC Richard was there talking to Eric, I of course in my hurry had forgotten to collect my wages.

"Hello Malc long time no see, you OK?" "Yeah fine Richard." As I have said before Richard was no longer a PC he had risen steadily through the ranks but unlike other career police officers he still regarded these few streets of ours as his manor and the people very much his family. Things were a lot quieter on the streets of W11 lately and I am sure much of that was down to Richard. Even in the bad times he had managed to maintain the respect and indeed co-operation of the locals be they black, white, English, Irish or any other make of man you could think of, I guess I hadn't thought of it before but, well he was a people person as they say nowadays.

"Eric, sorry to interrupt but you forgot to pay me." "No Malc you forgot to ask for it," that made Paul and Richard laugh and Richard put in his two-penn'oth. "Eric's right Malc, as they say you don't ask, you don't get," Richard looked at Eric and quipped, "mind you he is a polite lad now and I would like to take a certain amount of responsibility for that" and he smiled. Paul dipped into his money pouch gave me my wages and Eric told me to take a bit of produce as a perk. I of course didn't have to be told twice and put half a dozen apples in a bag; they were still my favourites and took me back to the early days when Eric tossed me an apple for my school lunch. "OK I'm off now, thanks lads" I chirped, "mind if I walk up with you Malc?" "No of course not Richard, I'd quite like that." He said goodbye to Eric and Paul and we wandered off chatting. "How's that young lady of yours Malc?" "Yeah she's really well, in fact that's why I'm rushing, she's coming over to mine tonight."

We wandered on and soon reached my house and Richard left me with a warning, I guess he saw the glint in my eye and he knew I could reach his hat much easier now. "Don't you dare I'll bloody arrest you if you do" and laughed, I didn't try to knock his hat off but I can tell you I sorely wanted to. "See you then Malc and say hello to your mum and dad for me."

A Life on the Lane

Sue came over about 6.30 pm; she had rung the door bell and for once for whatever reason I didn't hear it. Mum went down and let her in. It seemed weird, Sue knocked on my bedroom door and opened it; I was standing there singing at a transistor radio in just my underpants. Sue quipped "very nice Malc and I don't mean your singing." I grabbed my jeans and almost went flying in my haste to make myself decent and Sue just stood watching and smiling. She turned and closed the door and in the most tempting way you could imaging came over to me and closed her arms around me. "Oh Malc" it was a smouldering voice for a teenager but oh so sexy, "kiss me" she demanded and I of course obliged. She rubbed her hand up my bare back and over my shoulders, she caressed my chest in a way that no one had ever done before and I liked it, that fact would have been plainly obvious to Sue as she hugged me tightly. She pulled away and smiled "put your shirt on Malc in case your mum comes in." "I'm sorry Sue" I mumbled and she pulled me back in and while kissing me just said "no Malc I love you."

We sat on the floor with the transistor radio on and chatted and sure enough and good to her word mum knocked on the door, opened it and poked here head in. "Do you want a drink Sue?" she enquired, "Malc isn't much of a gentleman so he wouldn't ask. I've got some orange squash" mum said. "Thanks that would be lovely" Sue responded, I of course was ordered to the kitchen to collect it. When I returned Sue sat on the bed and I next to her, she whispered in my ear "I so want to wake up next to you Malc." I was again flabbergasted but I had exactly the same feelings "you don't mind waiting though do you Malc?" I was so relieved. Yes I wanted a sexual relationship as any youth my age but I kind of liked the respect the pair of us had, it just wasn't quite right at the moment. I steered the conversation on to my grandad, which after all that is why I got Sue to come over. I explained how I had just bonded with him and how my dad was so upset over his death.

"The other thing Sue was the army." Sue sat up straight, "don't worry Sue I ain't running off to join the foreign legion or anything, in fact it's quite the opposite. Grandad had a long chat with me some time back and I think he may have been trying to put me off joining up," Sue listened on intently. "He showed me stuff and told me things that made me question what I was thinking about, he told me about my dad too and I am sure that was as a result of their lunchtime chats, in other words I'm having second thoughts." Sue smiled "I can't say I'm sorry Malc, I never thought it was right for you anyway but I would never try to stop you doing what you want, I will support you in what- ever you decide." "But I've been telling everyone about my career plans and how I was going to be a great squaddie, what do I tell them now?" "Nothing Malc you don't need to tell anyone anything, just listen to your heart and make up your mind".

Sue and I cuddled and kissed and had the sort of evening courting couples all over the country have, our conversation drifted here and there and we laughed and smiled and not once did my mum come back in the room.

I walked Sue back over to her house and we sat on our steps by her front door, I didn't like actually leaving Sue but I did enjoy the process leading up to leaving. We kissed I put my jacket around her shoulders until it was time say goodnight. "Night Sue, I love you" "and I love you too Malc".

A Life on the Lane

CHAPTER 14
GROWN UP FEELINGS

Sunday morning was of course football day so off we went Sue, Me, Kit and Freddy. I Was a regular first team player by now, I enjoyed the role I had taken on, it suited me, maybe that is what made Mr. Collison such a good manager, he found the fit and put you in it, even the spotty kid became a star in the team, he moved up from midfield and I moved back a bit to cover him, he became a good old fashioned centre forward as you would call him these days. It wasn't only on a Sunday that our paths kept crossing. It turned out that John Collison was a Shepherd's Bush boy through to the marrow and what was more he bled blue and white, he had started coaching our school team and I have to say it was quite a team, I won't embarrass anyone by naming names but a few went on to really make the grade, even I had been good enough to train with QPR but circumstances dictated that Saturday mornings were for work not football so the school team was only a very special occasion.

Anyway that said Sunday was my time ... oh and Sue's so needless to say that meant football, meeting up with Rita and the others and a bloody good morning.

I picked up Sue and we started out for the rec, home games were good, we had started to gain a reputation as a tough team to beat and well even away, which usually meant the Scrubs, we didn't do too bad.

I was never made captain even though Mr. Collison relied on me to do an inordinate amount of shouting on the pitch; at training he always wanted me to take second group to do extra training on certain points of our game. I didn't mind but just sometimes I would have liked a little more recognition maybe.

The game was a good one, we had won in a convincing manner and to put the icing on the cake I had knocked one in. As I said before Jerry was really improving now he was getting service from the midfield and he got our other two, one either side of half time which Mr. Collison had always impressed on us was the most important time in a game. Before half time because the opposition find the half time break knocks their concentration and get in quick after half time before they get into their stride. On this Sunday Jerry exploited the situation perfectly. I'm not sure he had improved in his skills but his vision of the game and forethought were outstanding, I know because that's precisely what John had told me. John Collison may have been a professional footballer but as a manager, coach and people person he was the best. I had no idea why he hadn't gone on to be a manager at a professional

A Life on the Lane

football team so I asked him, "because I love the game and I love you kids running around on a Sunday morning and Wednesday evening. I've played for one of the best managers in the business and he didn't want to manage Liverpool, Spurs or even England, he stayed at a club he loved, win or lose". OK I thought that's good enough for me then.

After the game Sue and I walked back with Rita, Freddy and Kit. Bobby didn't seem too wrapped up with Rita and indeed she seemed to be having a good time joking around with Freddy. Sue whispered to me that "Reet and Bobby were letting things cool off." I have to say that although Bobby was a mate it would be nice to see Freddy enjoying himself, in a couple of words he deserved it.

As we all went our different ways I wandered over to Sue's house with her, we, as usual sat on the steps and chatted it was a bit of a debrief time for me, Sue had become something of a football expert lately and she had been observing everything especially if it involved me. "What do you want to do this afternoon Malc?" "Well if it doesn't rain too much why don't we walk up to Kensington Gardens?" "Oh yes I'd like that." "I'd better go then you know mum and her Sunday lunch, see you in about an hour." We had a brief kiss and off I went.

After dinner I went back to Sue's, she was out in a flash and off we went, we only got halfway and the heavens opened up, it absolutely poured down. We walked on a little and it just didn't seem to be improving. "Come on Malc it was a lovely idea but the weather is not getting better, let's go home." Still joking and laughing we splashed our way back to Sue's. "Come on in Malc, Mum and Dad aren't in we can get dried off and watch 'tele' for a while." "OK Sue suits me," so we went upstairs to Sue's flat. The West's flat had increased in size and quality since Peter had gone, it was now owned by a housing association and they maintained it and kept the number of tenants to the correct level. This was really good for local residents they seemed to stay in the properties for much longer, they enjoyed the security and safety the association meant.

As I said we went to Sue's flat and she fetched a towel from the bathroom, we had left our jackets dripping in the hallway. "Take that wet shirt of Malc," which I did without hesitation, as I have said before we were both so comfortable with each other and no sexual connotations were suggested with the exception of a little whispered "cor....!" from Sue, she could be really funny when she wanted. I took off my shirt and Sue towelled dry my back and chest, "oye" I said "don't you go enjoying that too much" we both laughed.

Sue went to the bathroom to dry herself and I was sent to her bedroom to wait for her. We had hung my shirt up to dry a bit in the kitchen and I wondered what her mum and dad would think if they came back now, but as what we thought of as a solid couple we were getting a lot more

A Life on the Lane

freedom and by definition trust. As I sat on Sue's bed waiting I flicked trough a copy of "Jackie" magazine. I have to say that reading some of the letters from the adolescent school girls it made me realise how lucky I was to have found Sue and she me of course.

Sue was in her dressing gown and went down and got us a drink of squash. She came back and put the drinks on the little table by the side of the bed. She went over to the dressing table she had in one corner of the room and took off her dressing gown and tossed it on to the bed, my chin nearly hit the floor, and she stood with her back to me in just a pair of briefs and brushed her hair. I couldn't help it I just wanted to hold her. I walked up behind her and put my hands on her hips. Sue didn't look round, she placed the brush on the dressing table and covered my hands with hers, and then to my amazement she raised both hands up her stomach and over her breasts. I cupped her gently in my hands. It felt so good, so warm and so natural, then she turned and lifted her arms around my neck and whispered "I love you so much it hurts, I want to be the person you wake up to every morning." We cuddled each other tight and it felt so good having our bare skin touching bare skin, I wanted that moment to last forever. I wanted so much to be a few years older, to be able to carry on.

Sue broke away and had a sip of her drink then turned opened the drawer of her dressing table and took out a bra. She didn't need to try and be sexy in the way she dressed, she just was, we didn't need to say anything we both knew that going any further was not the right thing for us at this time. I wouldn't sell that few seconds of watching her for any amount of money; it was so very precious to me.

Sue sat next to me on the bed and we laughed and joked, we read the letters out of her magazines and made comments about them, we had a fabulous time until Sue said "OK Malc time to go home I've got homework to do and I am sure you have to." It was a fabulous day and one I will never forget, life doesn't get any better I thought, and I am sure that at that particular time I was right.

After school on Monday I had decided not to go out but to just catch up on a bit of reading. I seemed to have such a busy schedule these days that it was getting to be something of a rarity. I had been hanging out with a couple of the lads from school for an hour or so as there didn't seem to be anything to rush for and I got back home just as mum was dishing up dinner and even Maureen was home from work.

Mum duly dished up dinner and dad chose that moment to give us the bombshell. As I have said Dad was getting a little itchy under the feet and felt that the time was getting there where he needed to move on in the job market and what with Grandad dying it must have just seemed right for him. "I've handed my notice in....." that was it, he then just ate his dinner.

A Life on the Lane

Malc being Malc, I was the first one to say something, "you're having a laugh dad." "No son I'm not, today I handed my notice in and in a week's time I start working for the GPO. It does of course mean we lose this flat, I've been to the housing association and we can move into a place in Wornington Road as soon as we want." I was flabbergasted, I knew Wornington Road and I'm certain that whatever we moved into wouldn't be very nice. That area skirted what were at some point the worst slums in the country, it was only the coming of the Westway and subsequent slum clearance that made the area half decent, with I should add the exception of Wornington Road which remained a bloody slum. "Malc I know it's not very nice but it's only temporary, they are doing up loads of houses and they promised this would be short term, and anyway if it isn't with what the governor has left, his house etc we will be able to buy our own place in a year or two, I just need to get established in the new job." "Why didn't you just wait dad in this job then we wouldn't need to move into temporary accommodation" Maureen added. "Look Mo I applied for this job sometime ago long before grandad died, I feel I need to improve our situation, what if I lost my job at anytime and was forced into moving maybe there wouldn't be any accommodation available, you Malc could end up in a home." As soon as he said that I thought of Paul, I knew I couldn't cope with that.

As the week went by sure enough we moved to Wornington Road, it was number 117 and for me this was

175

a very strange situation. I was sent to school from Westbourne Park Road and returned from school to Wornington Road. Now I'm not a snob by any means, I have seen poverty, I have had friends living in slums but I have to say this place took the biscuit. 117 Wornington Road was a large house divided into 3 flats but which had not been renovated yet. We were now in the same predicament in housing terms as many of my old friends. The kitchen was on the landing and we just had 1 bedroom and a living room come bedroom. The bath was in the public baths just over the other side of Mr. Brunel's railway lines and the windows draughty and falling apart.

The other main problem with this place was its location, it was in W10, again I'm not a snob but it was the other side of the Westway. Although the Westway was a raised motorway it's building completely divided a once vibrant community, I'm not a student of social history or anything so I have no idea why this was the case, maybe because so many more people were relocated from the W10 side of the motorway. People were unable for long periods to easily get between one area or the other so in the end just didn't bother, who knows? Not me.

The other problem was it was more of a distance between me and Sue, for whatever reason it really impacted on our relationship but worse was to come. After what I can only imagine was a couple weeks we had to bury grandad and he of course was to be laid to rest in Mortlake with my Nan.

A Life on the Lane

We all gathered at Grandad's, Dad had stayed there overnight with Uncle Bill, looking after him I like to think and I'm sure that dad would have had a good long chat with him, which was precisely what I was going to do. Mum, Maureen, Sue and I were taken to Thorpebank Road by Mo's boyfriend because we of course had the job of getting refreshments ready for the mourners. I have to say it suited me because I had time to talk to 'the Governor' in the front room alone. "Hi grandad" I whispered, maybe I just didn't want anyone else to hear, "I just wanted to tell you I've made up my mind about the army. I think I understood what you were trying to say. I'm not signing up, I know mum and dad will be happy, even Sue said she didn't think it was right for me and she means a lot to me. Anyway take a rest now grandad but can I ask you to look after Lin when you get to heaven. She's only young and I think she must be very lonely, I know you will look after her well, so thanks and say hello to Nan for me. I love you grandad, goodbye."

Over the next couple of hours everyone arrived to say their goodbyes and really give him a great send off. I listened to their stories and I was proud to hear about what a well loved and respected man he had been. Soon enough the cortege arrived and I knew it was time for his last journey

This of course was the same cemetery as where Lin was buried. Sue stayed with me and after the service it was her that suggested we go to Lin's grave, incredibly I never went to her grave over the years, I just didn't want to but Sue persuaded me and actually I'm glad she did.

After some hasty re-arrangements I was going to be taken home by Maureen's "new boyfriend" who I think was only roped in because he had a car. Sue and I went and found the grave and I saw her shed a tear after all she was her best friend but in true Sue style she said "I'll leave you here to chat Malc, don't rush." I had so many things I wanted to tell her, I wanted to ask her if it was OK for me to be with Sue, I told her we had moved and I told her that grandad was going to be looking after her now. I hadn't realised but I spoke out loud and I just told her "The Governor' was an old soldier, a war hero and if anyone would look after you it's him." After, well I don't know how long really Sue came up behind me and put her arm in mine, "it'll be alright Malc I talk to her all the time."

Sue and I wandered off to the car park and found our lift home, to my surprise Maureen was also in the car. "What you doing here?" Well I just thought I would leave mum and dad to get a bit of time alone that's all and of course me and Ian." I'm not sure if this was just a way of telling us his name or what but I got the message. I have to say Ian was a nice bloke actually and I thought he had potential, for Mo that is. The four of us headed back to Grandad's to meet all the family and friends but we had made our minds up not to hang around too long, I think Maureen and Ian had the same idea because after an hour or so they were conspicuous by their absence. "Mum

A Life on the Lane

would you be offended if I took Sue home now?" "Of course not, me and your dad are staying here tonight but Maureen will be home," "thanks mum." Mum kissed me on the cheek and then hugged Sue and gave her a kiss on the cheek too, "it's nice to have family around at times like this" Mum added.

As Sue and I left that cheeky little grin came to Sue's face, "did you hear that I'm family now?" "Yep you are Sue" I responded. As we left I repeated my mum's story and pointed out the missing finial on the porch, Sue's response was similar to mum's "that's the sort of thing you would bloody do Malcolm Williams." We laughed and headed off for Shepherd's Bush station, "2 singles to Ladbroke Grove please." I could not believe it there was I in my best bib and tucker and not a bloody penny in the pockets. "You tight bugger Malc you're always doing this." The big West Indian guy behind the counter laughed and said "you two newly-weds all done up in suits and tings, cos I'm honoured to be witness to your first domestic argument," and he laughed so loud. "No actually it was my grandad's funeral." The smile went from his face and he could not apologise enough, "there you go you two have dis one on London Underground." Sue persisted in trying to pay but he would have none of it. "Now get up de stairs, I hear de train coming."

Sue and I took a brisk climb up the stairs and sure enough the train was just coming down the tracks from Goldhawk Road, I wish I could really let you know the sound those trains made, they were noisy but somehow it was a very comforting noise, it meant getting home safely and hopefully on time, don't ask me why, it's stupid I know but the train always seemed more personal than the buses.

We got off at Ladbroke Grove and walked back up towards Wornington Road, we didn't say a lot we just walked really, and Sue had hold of my arm and was nicely tucked in to me keeping me as close as possible. When I say we didn't say much I'm not sure 2 words passed between us all the way up Ladbroke Grove, it wasn't until we went inside that Sue came alive. "You've been quiet was it something I said Sue?" "No I just thought with all the emotions of the day I'd keep quiet, I don't know why but it seemed right," I think actually it was more me than Sue I just didn't feel all happy and talkative, in fact I wished I had taken Sue straight home and then just come back to be on my own.

Maureen wasn't home and of course I knew she would be late but Sue and I just sat there barely a word passed between us I hadn't even bothered to get Sue a drink or anything and it wasn't really that long until she said "Malc I'd better get home now will I see you tomorrow?" "Yes of course I'll pop in after school." Sue grabbed her jacket and started down the stairs before I realised, "hey wait Sue I'll walk you home." "You don't have to Malc." "Sue, you're still my girlfriend and I know you would never forgive if I let you, and what's more Susan West, Malcolm Williams still loves you more than anything in the world."

A Life on the Lane

Sue cooed in her lovely sexy way and I apologised, she responded likewise. Maybe that's another little bit of growing up we need to do, learning to understand each other's feelings.

CHAPTER 15
MOVING ON

True to their word the housing association re-housed us within a few weeks; we were given a newly refurbished flat around the corner in Telford Road, Number 15. After the conditions we had lived in over the last few months Telford Road was luxury after all we had a bath and toilet of our own. We had the top 2 floors, an elderly what we now call gay theatrical gentleman had the ground floor flat and a middle-aged couple had the basement. I actually liked Telford Road but this had now caused more of a problem. Having accepted this newly refurbished property it meant we would not now be offered anything closer to Westbourne Park Road.

As I said this had impacted on Sue and me but we persevered with it, I think we did get closer mainly because it was harder for us. The amount we saw each other was nowhere near as much as we used to. Sure Sue would come up to my house and I still visited her after school but I now lived halfway to the rec and even closer to 'the Scrubs' so Sue would meet me at the game having walked up with Rita and Freddy, who were now an item.

A Life on the Lane

along with Kit and Bobby.

I remember seeing Rita and Bobby drifting apart because he hadn't bothered and how Freddy and her got together just on the walks from the games. I was beginning to think about things, was Sue enjoying her walks home with the others more than she should, I started to imagine things going on with her and Kit. I started to get really jealous, so jealous in fact that I even confronted Kit. Kit of course had no idea what I was on about but I still made it clear our friendship wasn't what it used to be. Sue got wind of what I'd said and wasn't pleased. It was so unusual, she just turned up one evening and we had it out. She was so upset that I could even think anything was or would go on. "Malc I love you, I always have, I would never do anything like that, and this is as hard for me as it is you. Sometimes when we don't see each other for a few days I sit in my room and cry, I just want to be with you, you and only you Malc." We both ended up in tears but this had been our first row, the first angry words we had said to each other ever.

Nothing really happened over the next few months, Sue and I stayed together, and it was still difficult we had a strong relationship; Sue would say that we would both be finishing school in a year or so and we could really sort ourselves out then, we could really make plans for the future. I even toyed with the idea of leaving school early and not doing my exams but Sue wouldn't hear of it, sometimes she was too sensible for her own good. "No

Malc you stay and do your exams, this is so important for our future. We are more than strong enough to get through this." I on the other hand wasn't so sure.

Dad came home from work one day with another of his great announcements, he and mum insisted one evening that Maureen and I be at dinner, what on earth was he up to. Well all was very clear soon enough, as we all knew at some point dad would try and secure a mortgage so that we could buy our own house, I knew he always wanted to after all mum's parents owned their own property as did her brother but I know that dad felt a little lacking in that area. He felt he had to be a home owner; certainly the government of the time kept pushing the fact that home ownership was the future.

At first I was quite grateful, I felt that this was when we could move back to W11, back home, back closer to Sue and all my mates but I was wrong. I had no idea about property prices etc. and it came as a bit of a shock when I found that we would in all probability be moving south of the river.

Mum's friend had not long since moved to the Croydon area which to me was another country or may as well have been, not only was it bloody miles away but it wasn't even on the underground network. To get from Croydon meant a main line train then two underground trains, what was I going to do?

I went and saw Sue and explained the situation, "don't

A Life on the Lane

you think we're strong enough Malc?" My first thought was if this doesn't work I'm going to get the blame. "Yes I... I am sure we are but it's going to be tough" I started thinking about the changes that would happen, different school for the last year or so, no more working down the lane and no more popping to Sue's. I had been having trouble seeing all my mates and Sue from just up the road so moving to Croydon seemed like moving to a different time zone.

I was lucky in the end that I was allowed to stay at Wren but for a teenager that journey got too much at times but I persevered. I got to see Sue when I could and she came to stay with us a few times but I guess it was inevitable really and through no one's fault we ended up going our separate ways.

I never got over Sue; it was the most loving relationship you could ask for. It was deep and passionate even though we never actually made love. Our petting, if you can call it that remained strictly above the waist, even though we were more than comfortable with each other's bodies. I never got over Sue in the same way as I never got over Lin but sometimes life does that to you, what was it Abdul used to say "Maktub," whatever it was I guess there is no point pushing against the universe because sure as eggs is eggs the universe will win.

Maureen I guess was the lucky one she married Ian, as I said from the start that lad had potential and I have to say we became pretty close. Mum got cancer and went through absolute hell for a few years before actually succumbing to it and Dad just carried on working.

Me...? Well I passed my exams and went on to college, I enjoyed a fine career in engineering and I met a girl and got married had a couple of great kids but in the long run it just didn't work out and we divorced. I stayed in touch with Freddy and Bobby but I got the feeling Kit never forgave me for the way I acted towards him when I accused him of playing around with Sue, I should have known that actually he was better than that and could not have been that way, I should have known he could have been one of my best friends. I did hear that he moved out to Milton Keynes or somewhere I never did speak to him again, which is one of my big regrets.

Sue... – She got a job in advertising and ended up marrying a high flier in the same firm. She also had two kids and gave up her career.

As I have said some mornings when you lay in your bath your mind just drifts, I had let myself drift on this sad day in a way I have never done in the bath before. Eric's death had a big impact on me and with today's funeral it was going to be a difficult thing to get through. He was going to be a great loss to many of us, he was always the first to help anyone and he would give anyone anything he had.

I was rudely awakened from my thoughts and indeed a

A Life on the Lane

rapidly cooling bath by my wife calling, "come on Malc you finished in that bath yet, we have so much to do and you're laying there daydreaming."

That was it I knew better than ignore her, I was fully aware that we had to get across London and I hated rushing as did Sue.

CHAPTER 16
NEW BEGINNING

Oh did I forget that bit? Yes that was Sue, well I guess you are wondering how that happened, well back a few years ago Freddy had called me out of the blue, we had kept in touch, you know the usual Christmas card or the odd bit of news now and again but not on a particularly regular basis, then he called which I found unusual after all it wasn't Christmas, far from it.

"Hello Malc, its Freddy, you doing OK?" The conversation went on a bit but I knew he hadn't called just for a chat. "Listen Malc me and Rita (yes they married and stayed as a couple), well we've arranged a bit of a get together for our anniversary, nothing special we'd really like to see you." I am not really a social person since I got divorced I just sort of enjoyed my own company but on this occasion somehow I managed to let Fred persuade me. Freddy now lived in Hitchin so it was a fair trot to get there, so of course it meant booking a hotel etc. I really wasn't sure if I wanted the bother but as I said Freddy and indeed Rita were very persuasive and I agreed, reluctantly. "You'll enjoy it Malc, Bobby's coming so it's bound to be

A Life on the Lane

entertaining."

Sure enough the day of Freddy and Rita's anniversary came and I made the journey up to Hertfordshire, it was a lovely summer's day and it was actually a very pleasant drive. When I got there I went to the hotel and checked in, it was only a Travelodge but it was a bed which was all I needed.

The get together was in a restaurant a couple of miles from the hotel so I booked a taxi. It was a lovely restaurant and because I really didn't want to stay too long or late I got there early, sure enough Freddy and Rita were there and I was glad to see the years really hadn't been too rough on them. Freddy was just as he was the last time I had seen him and Rita was just beautiful, she had really matured into a lovely lady.

Right on cue and in his own inimitable way Bobby came in as we were gathering at the bar; he came over like we had seen each the day before. "Hello Malc you OK? Still playing football?" I think in Bobby's head because he hadn't seen me in such a long time, time had stood still, I was still a teenager walking up to the rec on a Sunday morning. "No Bobby I'm too old for all that now." "Funny" said Bobby "I thought we were the same age and I'm still playing." About this point in the conversation a lady walked up to Bobby and said "you going to introduce your friend Bob?" "Oh yes of course, Malc this is my wife Mary." "Hi Mary I'm Malcolm your husband and I go way back," "anyway good to see you Malc but Mary says we have to mingle," and with that they went. I know who wears the trousers there I thought, but to be honest I think that is exactly right for him.

After about half an hour or so it seemed to me that everyone that was coming was already here, then the door opened. You could have knocked me down with a feather because walking straight towards me was Sue. She looked absolutely stunning in a black dress and super high heels. I had said goodbye to her long ago as a girl but here in front of me was a woman and she looked fabulous. I expected her to be followed in by some city whizz kid husband but she was alone, as she approached I didn't know what to do, I of course still loved her dearly, I had never and would never get over her.

"Hello Malc you OK?" Sue continued as my mouth didn't seem engaged to my brain and that old wobbly feeling I hadn't felt since we were teenagers came back. "Yeah I'm erm yeah OK." I couldn't help it I just blurted it out. "Sue you look amazing but where's your husband?" Before she could answer Rita and Freddy came over, Rita hugged Sue like the old friends they were and Freddy managed to squeeze in a polite peck on her cheek. Come on over here you two now everybody's here we can sit down. Sure enough Sue and I had seats together I raised the courage to ask her if she wanted a drink, it was strange I had only ever known her drink orange squash "a nice glass of white wine would be good Malc" Sue responded.

A Life on the Lane

We had a great evening; I think because to be honest I only concentrated on one person, I really don't think our eyes left each other for the whole event. I didn't ask her about herself and she didn't have to ask about me, she seemed to know everything there was to know, she knew I had a family, she knew I was divorced she even knew I had a career in engineering, the only time I learned anything about her was when she told me she too was divorced and what's more it was very recent. We ate dinner, not that I did, I just picked at the food and had a drink or two, of course as with all alcoholic festivities as the evening went on the conversation got easier. Sue and I hadn't left each other's side all night and when she suggested we go somewhere quieter I just couldn't wait. Sue said her goodbyes as did I, and we left the restaurant.

It was a lovely summer evening and we decided to amble down the road to a pub it felt so good when Sue put her arm in mine and snuggled in, "bring back memories Malc?" "Yes it certainly does, you know I never got over you don't you?" "Malc neither did I get over you but I'm sure you knew that though." We found a pub and went inside but to be honest neither of us wanted to drink it wasn't long before Sue said "take me home Malc" I wasn't sure what I had done wrong but I thought she was probably right. The pub landlord called a cab for us and true to his word it arrived within minutes. When it did I said to Sue "where are you staying tonight?" "Well my clothes are at Rita and Freddy's but I guess I can pick them up in the morning, tonight Malcolm Williams I'm staying at your hotel" she said. I was flabbergasted and a little embarrassed, this was the first time outside of business that I had stayed in a Travelodge, I could have kicked myself why did I not book a decent hotel I thought, "I'm so sorry it's just a Travelodge Sue." "I really don't care it could be an old barn for all it matters I'm here for you not the decor." OK I thought let's just relax and let the evening unfold.

We got to the hotel in a few minutes and I paid the driver, I still wasn't sure what to expect after all Sue was in the driver's seat on this one. When we got to the room I still wasn't sure what to expect, everything was so surreal but as was her way Sue was in control, it seemed ironic only hours earlier I had commented on Bobby's wife wearing the trousers.

In the room I made a coffee and we sat on the bed chatting, I really was on cloud nine, then Sue stood up moved over to the mirror and let her hair down, it was longer now than I ever remember but it was good. Her hair flowed down over her neck and formed waves over her shoulders, Sue turned to me and unbuttoned my shirt, she slid it down my shoulders and cooed in that oh so sexy way of hers "Malcolm Williams don't you say anything I have dreamt about this moment for years so DO NOT spoil it." "Me...?"

She turned to the mirror again and run her fingers through her hair then to my amazement unzipped her dress

A Life on the Lane

dropped it down and stepped out of it. She turned and oh so coolly tossed it on the bed, she stood there in her briefs and I came to my senses and realised that this was a replay of that rainy day in her bedroom, all of a sudden I knew exactly what I had to do. I stood up and walked up behind her placed my hands on her hips and waited. Sure enough as I recalled every move she played this exactly to the script. She put her hands over mine, raised them up over her stomach and over her breasts. I stood there with her breasts cupped oh so gently in my hands and all the feelings of the previous years flooded back; Sue turned and raised her arms over my head and round my neck. She looked deep into my eyes and whispered "Malcolm Williams you are still the person I want to wake up to for the rest of my life and the rest of my life starts tonight" and it certainly did. She put her arms around my neck and kissed me, her tongue probed my mouth and we cuddled. I guess I knew that this time we wouldn't say goodnight and go to separate houses, tonight was ours and Sue intended to make the most of it, and I should say so did I.

We sat on the end of the bed and kissed and kissed and kissed, I just couldn't stop and if you asked me the time I would have no idea, to me all the numbers on the clock face said one thing, Sue time and I really didn't want it to end. We managed to remove the remainder of our clothes and slid under the covers, I can't explain but I thought this just felt like the first time, even though I had 2 kids and been married it felt like wiping the slate clean and starting afresh. I had never through the years wanted anyone else,

I can't comprehend why or how we had split up, it was simply crazy and I was thinking, no hoping, this was the same for her.

We spent a wonderful night together and made love like I had never done before because this really was love, in the morning Sue was just looking at me, "good morning Malc I woke up earlier and what's more I woke up next to you, you are the first person I have seen today." I looked into Sue's eyes; they had that happy love for life look about them. She looked back at me and in the voice that I have always adored she whispered "Malc can we do it again" we laughed and that was it we just couldn't help ourselves. We made love again with what I thought was impossible, more passion.

As we lay there in the afterglow of this magic sexual union she whispered in my ear "Malc you are the first person I have seen this morning, I have got my wish and woken up next to you but it was so good to be the person you made love to."

After just laying there for a while we knew we had to get ready to leave, but there was still one thing that Sue had on her agenda. She went into the bathroom for a shower and as soon as she felt ready she called, "Malc, come and wash my back." I didn't need to be asked twice. I got in the shower behind her, she turned and with the water tumbling down over our heads we kissed. Sue knew how to use her body and she certainly knew how to get me in a

A Life on the Lane

lather with her soap expertise. It was a morning I never wanted to end.

After grabbing a cup of coffee I drove Sue to Freddy and Rita's still wearing her high heels and little black dress, I was surprised to see them up and about, wide eyed and bushy tailed, "cup of coffee Malc?" Freddy asked - "ummm yeah, please." It was as if nothing had happened and I think I twigged at that point. "This was all planned wasn't it?" "Well now you're asking yes it was." Freddy took me out to the garden and we sat on the patio. "You guessed that Rita and Sue have phoned each other almost on a daily basis and well we all knew you two had never got over each other. Sue's marriage was a sham and she was unhappy from day one, so last night seemed like a good time to get you two together again. Malc when Sue turned up here yesterday she was smiling, it's the first time I have seen the old Sue for years and well when I went outside the restaurant to meet her, I told her you were there and the smile on her face was just huge. Malc don't let her go again if any couple were meant to be it was you two" and he left me outside by myself. I didn't really need Freddy's advice I already knew that this time I wouldn't let Sue go, one thing I am good at is learning from my mistakes and this time I felt I had been given a second chance.

I drove Sue back to her house which was somewhere near Heathrow, I am not sure how she explained it to her children but they seemed to know it was right. Sue introduced us and they had a knowing look, "Malc this is Amanda and Malcolm, don't worry they know all about you." I took a sharp intake of breath, "everything...?" I questioned. Amanda was so like her mum and replied for her." Oh yes we know all about you" and she came over and cuddled me, I was so relieved.

Without going into details that night was the only night we have spent apart since, Sue's children and mine get on really well, we of course have a house of our own now and you can count the times I have met Sue's ex on the fingers of one hand. He really wasn't a nice person and even the children were aware they were not the product of a loving relationship, their visits to him were few and far between and we all became very close. It may be a space age family but I really could not wish for anything better.

But to bring this all back to the day ahead, again Sue woke me from my daydreams. "Malc get out of that bloody bath ....now or we are going to be late." "Yes Sue, come and dry my back." Sue of course came straight away and I knew exactly what to expect, which is of course why I asked." Sue opened the bathroom door and cooed, "I love you Malcolm Williams" "and I love you Susan Williams"

A Life on the Lane

CHAPTER 17
A FITTING END

Eric's son, Lin's brother had arranged everything and he came to me first which was such an honour, "Malc thanks for coming Dad would never have forgiven me if you hadn't. He thought of you as a son and sometimes even more than me." "That's certainly not the case Stewart, yeah I know you were all more than family to me but you and Lin were always his family." Stewart pulled me to one side, "Malc you were a brother to me, I never expected you and Lin to be apart but if anyone is a replacement it's Sue, Sue was more than family as well so it's not like we aren't all family, but don't be a stranger, I couldn't handle that again."

I had never tried to replace Eric's family and now I guess it was time to face Eric's widow, again Jean had been a second Mum to me but I now had to lay a few ghosts to rest. Sue stayed back and I approached her, "Jean I am so sorry, this is a day I never ever wanted to face but its here, so we should cope. I don't know what to say but can I have a hug?" She looked up at me and just said, "does my son really have to ask, no one that knew you Malc ever got over you, and just be sure Eric is with you," "and Lin, I will never forget her and my failing to protect her" I responded. "I always blamed myself for what happened. I always felt that if I hadn't suggested meeting her at the school gate maybe she wouldn't have got held behind with me. She would have been safely in your flat when Michael and Peter arrived not on the stairs. Jean I am so sorry" "Malcolm it wasn't your fault there is only one person to blame, now let that be an end to it" I had of course confessed my feelings of guilt to Sue a long time ago and she had said the same but until I had told her family I still carried that guilt. My only regret was that it was too late to tell Eric. Jean must have read my mind because she went on to say that "Eric had the same feeling of guilt, he always wanted to tell you Malc."

"Malc bring Sue over before it gets too hectic it would be so nice to have ALL my family around me at least once more."

No one but no one from our community shunned anyone; there were enough locals to make this the most W11 gathering I had ever known. Words fail me and enough has probably been said, Jean asking for Sue was just her way of saying what had gone on was acceptable and if you like I was forgiven. I made an oath to myself to never forget anyone again I would make a conscious decision to be there for anyone, just as Eric was.

Eric's funeral got underway in exactly the fashion it was supposed to. Outside his house was a market traders handcart and for the first part of his journey Eric was going back down the Lane for the last time, this was all that he ever wanted and all of us had gathered just to witness this event. Even though Eric had been retired for years the whole market came to a standstill, just like earlier times men doffed their hats and everyone stood still both costermongers and their customers, everyone gave this very big man the respect and reverence he so richly deserved. At the top of the market almost outside Colville school Eric was transferred to the hearse and those that had gone along the lane filled the cars in the cortege. It was such a dignified occasion and even with the toing and frowing of the mourners nothing detracted from why we were here.

The funeral carried on to Mortlake and Eric was finally laid to rest with Lin in their family plot. I walked Jean down to that plot and realised how frail she was, she looked at me and whispered "we will soon be a family again; it won't be long before I join them." All I could say was "no you have years left in you" but deep down I knew that wasn't what she wanted. "No Malc I'm ready." That was the last words we had, I never spoke to her again, I don't think she lasted more than six months after Eric died, I just think that was real love.

I met some other people that day that have been massive in my life, people that could have been forgotten and it was me that would have been poorer for it.

Paul was there as you would expect, he had come with his wife. He hadn't changed and again the years had been good to him, we had a very close relationship without really being close if that makes sense. Paul came over to me and hugged me. "It's good to see you tiddler" he said "I know you have all that you deserve Malc, you look after that little lady of yours, and you're a lucky man." Paul had taken over the stall from Eric and even in his later life he carried on. He had a family now and I felt that even for him his life had turned out OK.

The other person that arrived totally unannounced was Kit, I really hadn't expected to see him but here he was in front of me. I wasn't sure how he would accept me but time is a great healer. I had just two words for him and he knew they came from the heart, "I'm sorry" again we hugged and I knew everything was OK.

That was about it really because after all this wasn't about me but one thing really was too much for my emotions. Someone had slipped in and kept metaphorically to the shadows, I hadn't recognised the big man at the back of the service, maybe I just wasn't looking but this was a big man that I owe so much to. He was second only to Eric in protecting me and helping me even when I didn't think I needed help. He had retired many years previously and to be honest I had never thought of him as anything other than a Police officer but Richard had been more of a mentor than I can say. He protected me, he helped me and when

A Life on the Lane

necessary he scolded me, but over the years I grew to love that man. I just went up to him and shook his hand, "good to see you Malc even on such a sad day." I looked up at him and just had to quip "you could have worn that pointy hat just once more Richard, you know just for old time's sake." "You cheeky bugger." He almost bent to hug me because of our height difference; it was good and just reaffirmed our bond. I just had to tell him how much he meant to me, "Richard I owe you so much not least of all my life, if not for you that night in the canal would have ended so differently, Thank you." "Yeah I know but Tom never did forgive me for pushing him in after you" we both laughed.

We had gathered at a local hostelry to say goodbye to Eric and somehow I had got through today, I had replayed my life from those moments spent in my bath this morning to meeting all my friends and family here at Eric's celebration. It was over now and as with all that has made the modern world what it is today Sue and I could drive home and get over the excitement, trauma or whatever we should call today.

As we drove home Ralph McTell's Streets of London came on the radio, Sue was singing along "Malc I can see all of those people in this song, the old man, the old girl, all of them. It's Portobello Road in a song" "it is love and I always think of the people down the lane too but here's an ironic fact, that song was written about Surrey Street market in Croydon, our adopted home and where we will be shortly" "Really" was Sue's only response.

"Ahh home sweet home, it's so nice to close our door behind us and lock the world outside" Sue remarked.

We had a welcome cup of coffee and Sue told me that Jean had slipped her something for me as a reminder of Eric, not that I needed it he was etched deep within me. Jean had given Sue the pocket watch, chain and charm, I had always admired Eric's watch chain but the charm was new to me. "Jean said you had always liked his watch chain and he always said it was yours when he was gone, she gave it to me to save you getting upset, and she was more than pleased it was coming to you Malc." When I saw it I was nearly in tears, it was a heart shaped charm and it was engraved "Lin" and her date of birth and death, I don't know how I kept my tears in. "Why didn't she give it to me Sue?" "She wanted to make sure it was OK with me but you know that has never been a problem, when Lin died Malc they gave me her jewellery box as I have told you, I know you will want to use the chain Malc but I really think our little treasure chest would be a good home for it but you decide." "No your right Sue, but let's go to bed now."

After that and on a final note Sue had a few words to say tonight as she does every single night, "Goodnight Malc, you're the only person I want to wake up next to, tomorrow and every morning, I love you Malc Williams." "And I love you Susan Williams." Goodnight.

THE END

A Life on the Lane

<u>Acknowledgements</u>

I am not one to fill pages with dedications but in these few lines I will just highlight one or two.

I want to thank my Wife Linda, she puts up with my tap tap on the laptop constantly.

My Facebook group of friends who have featured in characters within these pages, you know who you are.

Susan and her Family thank you for lending me your personalities.

Jamie Franklin who donated the sketches

Maureen Binstead for her work in sorting out the mess I made of typing this work out.

And in the best tradition of radio dedications "Anyone else that knows me"

Thank you

Melvin Wilkinson

Melvin was born in Shepherd's Bush but was raised in Notting Hill from a very early age and even though he now lives in rural Wiltshire he still looks upon London W11 as his spiritual home. Notting Hill and Dale are his roots and he considers it the most important area he has lived in. "I love Notting Hill and where ever I am in the world I am not happier than I am in returning to W11"

Melvin is the author of the best selling social history book "The book of Notting Hill (A very special part of London" a part of the Halsgrove Parish History Series. ISBN:- 1 84114 508 4   ISBN:- 978 1 84114 508 2

A Life on the Lane is a new chapter in his literary portfolio; it is his first foray into the world of fiction.

Printed in Great Britain
by Amazon